Thank you, Ral... **words. Thank yo**... **the loss of her fa**... **failed to do. Thank you for helping me every step of the way.**

The words thundered in Clarinda's mind, pushed out of the way by a realization as heady as air that has turned to steam in the heat.

I love Ralph.

The thought rampaged from the toes of her sandaled feet to the kerchief she wore to cover her hair. She felt as if her feelings must be branded on her forehead, but no one said a thing, as if it was just another Saturday morning in Maple Notch.

"I was thinking we could put the beans over here next to the fence." At least she assumed that was what he was saying. The words flying through her head consisted of things like *love and joy, sunshine and warmth, comfort and peace.*

How Ralph could remain so near her and not know how she felt seemed impossible. What thoughts hid behind his helpful exterior? Was it possible that all the time they had spent together the past six months had more to it than supporting the war effort and leading their town?

Books by Darlene Franklin

Love Inspired Heartsong Presents

Hidden Dreams
Golden Dreams
Homefront Dreams

DARLENE FRANKLIN

Award-winning author and speaker Darlene Franklin
lives in Oklahoma near her son's family. Darlene loves
music, needlework, reading and reality TV. She has over
twenty books published, including three previous titles
about Maple Notch, Vermont. She's a member of both
American Christian Fiction Writers and Oklahoma City
Christian Fiction Writers.

You can find Darlene online,
at darlenefranklinwrites.blogspot.com
and www.facebook.com/darlene.franklin.3. You may
also be interested in her Facebook group, Darlene's
5 Questions a Day, where she will answer the first five
questions related to the writing life posed on any given
day. Group members are also welcome to contribute.

DARLENE FRANKLIN

Homefront Dreams

#1077

HEARTSONG
PRESENTS

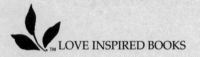

LOVE INSPIRED BOOKS

Recycling programs
for this product may
not exist in your area.

ISBN-13: 978-0-373-48688-5

HOMEFRONT DREAMS

Copyright © 2014 by Darlene Franklin

All rights reserved. Except for use in any review, the reproduction
or utilization of this work in whole or in part in any form by any
electronic, mechanical or other means, now known or hereafter
invented, including xerography, photocopying and recording, or in
any information storage or retrieval system, is forbidden without
the written permission of the editorial office, Love Inspired Books,
233 Broadway, New York, NY 10279 U.S.A.

This is a work of fiction. Names, characters, places and incidents are
either the product of the author's imagination or are used fictitiously, and
any resemblance to actual persons, living or dead, business establishments,
events or locales is entirely coincidental.

This edition published by arrangement with Love Inspired Books.

® and TM are trademarks of Love Inspired Books, used under license.
Trademarks indicated with ® are registered in the United States Patent
and Trademark Office, the Canadian Trade Marks Office and in other
countries.

www.Harlequin.com

Printed in U.S.A.

Wherefore take unto you the whole armour of God,
that ye may be able to withstand in the evil day,
and having done all, to stand.
—*Ephesians* 6:13

Like the youngest daughter in this story, Anita Finch, my mother (Anita Bremner) was nine years old when the Japanese bombed Pearl Harbor. Mom went home to be with the Lord four years ago, but her memories of World War II form the heart of *Homefront Dreams*. To you, Mom, celebrating with me in heaven's grandstands.

Chapter 1

Maple Notch, Vermont, November 3, 1942

Darkness had fallen by the time the polls at Maple Notch Town Hall closed. From the front porch of the female seminary across the town square, Clarinda Tuttle Finch watched the doors close with anxiety in her heart. Ten months had passed since she had accepted the position as the mayor pro tem when her beloved Howard had enlisted in the army. No one expected that three months later he would be dead, a casualty of this new world war the United States was fighting.

When the time for the next election came, Clarinda surprised herself as much as everyone else by deciding to run on her own merits. She faced a worthy opponent, Ralph Quincy, the high school principal. His entourage held court in front of the general store around the corner from the seminary. The town's youth supported him, and their excitement could be heard from this distance. If Clarinda wasn't running for reelection, her eldest daughter, Betty, a high school senior, would probably join them.

But Clarinda's only child old enough to vote was her firstborn, and he was fighting Hitler's hordes in Europe. Closing her eyes briefly against the ever-present pain and worry, she sent up a quick prayer for Howard Jr.

"Mom?" Her second son, Arthur, had come home for the night from the University of Vermont, a short distance away in Burlington. "Mr. Smith called. They've tabulated the votes."

Clarinda didn't ask about the results. They wouldn't make the announcement until the candidates arrived at the town hall. Win or lose, she would learn the outcome at the same time as everyone else. Putting a hand to her throat, she took a deep breath to steady her nerves. "Very well, then."

She clapped her hands together. "May I have everyone's attention?" She used what she called her "Aunt Flo voice," one that commanded respect. "They are ready to announce Maple Notch's new mayor."

Arthur walked beside her, and her three daughters led the group of her supporters. Mr. Quincy's group approached the town hall at the same time, while Mr. Smith took a spot at the top of the steps.

"Citizens of these United States in the township of Maple Notch in the state of Vermont, you have chosen the person you wish to lead us through the dark days ahead, days when we who remain fight the war at home. It is my privilege as former mayor of our upstanding community to announce the results." Mr. Smith paused, drawing out the drama of the moment.

Smith was as pompous as he was good-hearted. Back

in 1938, he had bowed out as mayor after two terms, and Howard had been elected.

Arthur touched Clarinda's shoulder, urging her to move forward. Ralph had already left his contingent and taken his place in front of Mr. Smith.

"The mayor of Maple Notch for these next four years is…"

Someone on Mr. Quincy's side of the steps thrummed a snare drum, and Clarinda's insides twisted with each beat.

"…Clarinda Tuttle Finch!"

A smile burst from inside out. *Thank You, Lord.*

A smiling Ralph—and goodness, his smile seemed as genuine as hers was—shook her hand. "Congratulations, Clarinda." He stepped back, leaving the way open for her to climb the steps to the porch.

"Madam Mayor, congratulations." Mr. Smith bowed over her hand.

"Smile, Mrs. Finch!" Rusty Henshaw shouted as Mr. Smith shook her hand and the camera light flashed. The dark blue dress, with tailored collar and a thin black belt, and the veil of her hat covering her forehead should look well in the picture.

Clarinda took her place behind the microphone. "Citizens of Maple Notch! Thank you for the privilege of serving as your mayor for the next four years."

Cheers broke out at that statement, including Ralph's supporters. Judging by the smile on his face, no one would guess he had lost.

"Some people call this a dark time. We face implacable opponents on all sides. Valiant men have already fallen in the battle against the enemies of freedom and democracy, my own husband among them." Her voice caught, and she was astute enough to recognize the power her personal loss gave her within the community.

"For the next four years, I will strive to continue the legacy of my husband, Howard Finch. I promise to be strong in the face of adversity, to fight the war at home, and to give of myself, my friends and family, and if necessary, my life, for the cause of freedom." She pointed to a couple standing in front on her side of the steps. "Joe and Jane Johnson lost their boy at Guadalcanal only a few weeks ago. And over there, there's an empty place at the Simpsons' table these days." As she mentioned those who served and those who had died, a somber mood fell across the crowd. "I salute those who put their lives on the line."

Applause broke out at the appeal to patriotism. She decided to lighten the mood. "My grandmother Clara Farley Tuttle—"

Laughter rippled through the crowd. Clarinda always found a way to mention Grandma Clara in her speeches, which tickled her listeners.

"—would have been proud of the young women in our community who have chosen to serve overseas." As she mentioned them by name, she took pleasure in noting to herself how many of them had graduated from the seminary her grandmother had founded.

"We dedicate ourselves anew this day to the cause of freedom, to the defense of democracy, to the support of those who fight on the front lines. Years ago, when the United States faced another enemy in a different war, Francis Scott Key saw the flag flying and wrote words that I still treasure today. 'Oh! thus be it ever, when freemen shall stand/Between their loved home and the war's desolation./Blest with victory and peace, may the Heav'n rescued land/Praise the Power that hath made and preserved us a nation.'"

After quoting the remaining words of the last verse, Clarinda said, "Join me in singing the national anthem."

* * *

Keep smiling, Ralph reminded himself as they sang. He had great respect for Clarinda Tuttle Finch. Who didn't? She had not only borne the loss of her husband with grace, she had taken hold of the reins of government of Maple Notch with a firm hand. Under her leadership, she had eased the transition from peaceful village to a stanchion of democracy on the home front. Also she was Maple Notch born and bred, counting her ancestors among the founders of the town, a fact that mattered a lot around here.

The past was the problem, though. She held on to it with cement gloves, at least regarding the old-fashioned school her family ran. Even the name, the Maple Notch Female Seminary, sounded antiquated in 1942. The century had moved forward, and the town needed to move with it. Although he was close in age to the esteemed mayor, he faced the future head-on. When he ran for mayor, he knew he fought an uphill battle against not only an incumbent but also a respected war widow.

When the song ended and the applause died down, Ralph greeted Clarinda at the bottom of the steps. "Congratulations again. But you haven't seen the last of me yet."

"I know." She raised her chin, calm eyes regarding him from behind the veil over her forehead. "You still hold your seat on the town council. I'll see you at our next meeting if not before then at church."

Yes, you will. He nodded and walked away, allowing her supporters to rush forward. The people had spoken, and he would continue working for change from his position on the council.

Rich Adams, the town druggist and one of Ralph's biggest supporters, met him as he crossed the square in the direction of the general store. As another council member,

Rich knew Ralph's intentions better than anyone else. "Do you think we stand a chance?"

Ralph shrugged. "While there's life, there's hope." He took a step forward. "Let me thank my faithful workers before we worry about the council."

"Mr. Quincy." A bright female voice called, probably one of his students.

Ralph turned around. Betty Finch, the new mayor's eldest daughter, waved. She would have been at his high school if not enrolled at the seminary. "Yes, Betty?"

Betty's light brown hair curled around her face, and she was peppy enough to be on the cheerleading squad, if the seminary had one. She was smart, too, like all the other Finch children.

"I thought you ran a good campaign. I like some of your ideas." She put her hand over her mouth, as if afraid of what else might come out. "I love Mom, but I don't always agree with her." She glanced over her shoulder, where her brother Arthur waited for her. "I have to go. I'll see you later."

"A spy in the enemy's camp." Rich's thin lips curved in a smile. "You always did make an impression on the girls."

The two men walked in the direction of the store. Ralph had known Rich all his life, had fought by his side in the trenches of France. Rich had envied Ralph's reputation as a Valentino when they had roomed together at college after the war. Only Rich had married his college sweetheart, while Ralph had lost the only woman he had ever really loved during the 1918 flu pandemic. Plenty of women had pursued him over the years, but no one had caught his interest.

He and the mayor had that in common. Life had stripped

them both of the persons they loved. They wouldn't be the last ones to lose someone before this war ended.

"Betty's high-spirited," Ralph said. "She reminds me of her aunt Winnie Sawtelle. From what I hear, Betty's sister Norma is a lot more like Clarinda."

"And you always did like the serious types," Rich said. They arrived at the store and were greeted by light applause.

Ralph waited a few seconds for the dejected crowd to stop clapping. "I can't thank you enough for your support over the course of my campaign. I will continue to fight for the causes we believe in, as part of the town council."

Rich raised his glass of punch in support of the idea.

"But join me in supporting Mayor Finch as we move forward in the war effort. We may disagree on the details, but we are united in wanting a strong America to fight for freedom and democracy for those under the thumbs of our enemies."

Fresh applause broke out. If the race had depended on rhetoric alone, Ralph might have won. "Stay awhile. Finish up the cake and punch. You gave this campaign everything you had, and you deserve to celebrate."

He thanked each volunteer personally. How did a candidate for an office like the presidency ever thank the people who helped get him elected? *We may have lost the battle... but the war is far from over.*

Nine days after the election, Clarinda prepared for the bimonthly town-council meeting with renewed energy. The citizens of Maple Notch had returned her to office, a privilege she didn't take lightly. The election had been closer than she'd hoped; a mere eleven votes separated her from Ralph.

The town council consisted of eight members, and she

only voted in the case of a tie. Tonight's agenda began with an easily resolved matter—approval of additional funds for clearing snow.

The controversial business of the evening would arise under New Business—the renewal of the Maple Notch Female Seminary's charter as a school. After being a successful, *vital* part of the life of Maple Notch for more than 150 years, the seminary faced serious opposition to its renewal.

The source of the opposition distressed her: Ralph Quincy, her opponent in the mayoral race. The high school principal should be pleased that leaders across New England came from a school located in their small town and should not want to close its doors.

Clarinda could pick up the phone and call professors at all Seven Sisters schools, not to mention a host of smaller colleges, who were seminary alumnae. She could name half a dozen other graduates involved in politics as mayors or members of congress. One of them had even been appointed to a vacant senate spot when the woman's husband had died. How could anyone deny the importance of continuing such a distinguished tradition?

Clarinda looked at the blank space underneath the line for the school's charter, wondering if anyone else would bring up New Business.

Ten years ago, when Clarinda had given birth to her youngest child, Anita, Clarinda had never envisioned herself working anywhere besides the family farm. When Anita had started school, Howard had run for mayor. Clarinda found herself involved more and more in running the town, first as Howard's secretary, then as mayor herself.

Clarinda and Anita had moved into the Bailey Mansion

the previous September. As boarding students, her older girls, Norma and Betty, already lived there.

Clarinda retired to the suite she kept as her own to freshen up for the night. She wanted to look her best. Howard used to say she looked a little bit like Joan Crawford. She lifted her hand to her cheek. The edges had softened through the years. Her once dark hair was now gray, at places fading into white. The padded shoulders of her navy blue dress, the belted waistline, the tailored look of her jacket suited her outlook these days. When she added glasses and well-defined eyebrows, she projected an image of no-nonsense intelligence.

Someone knocked at the door, and Betty came in. "Stop primping, Mom. You look fine."

"I'm not primping." The words jumped to Clarinda's lips. Ridiculous thought that a woman of forty-five with mostly gray hair should care about her appearance.

"You've been in here for fifteen minutes, and you chase me out of the bathroom if I spend that much time in front of a mirror." Betty flopped down on top of the bed. "You don't start your next term as mayor until January, you know."

"I know." Clarinda fiddled with a diamond earring that Howard had given her on their twentieth anniversary. "But since there are no new members coming on board the town council, we might as well get to work. Would you help me with my earrings, please?"

Betty pushed the stud onto the end of the earring before brushing the curls around Clarinda's face. "You're beautiful. You should start dating, you know."

In the mirror, Clarinda saw her mouth open. "Elizabeth Clara Finch, whatever do you mean?"

"You know. You, and a man, alone, without all of us hanging on." Betty took the silver rat, the padding, from the top of Clarinda's head, brushed her curls away from her face, then repositioned the rat neatly, adding height above her carefully drawn eyebrows. "Someone like, I don't know, Principal Quincy?"

An image of distinguished gray hair and brandy-colored eyes flashed through Clarinda's mind, but she ignored it. "There will never be anyone for me except your father. Principal Quincy is a fellow concerned citizen, that is all, and we don't even agree about simple things, like education."

Betty straightened her lips as she continued pinning Clarinda's hair.

The dinner bell rang, and they headed downstairs. "Be sure you get your homework done."

Betty frowned. "I'm not a baby. You don't even know what I do at night when you're not here."

Clarinda took in a deep breath. Betty was giving her more trouble than both her sons together had. "I know." She hugged her daughter, and they went to the dining room to eat with the students.

After dinner, Clarinda put on her winter coat, black wool with a lining of gray taffeta and a fur collar, and walked through the back door into the crisp cold air. The temperature hovered around freezing, with a hint of snow in the air. She and Howard used to enjoy walking under the moon together on nights like this. *Oh, Howard. If you were here...* She never thought she would want to relive the 1930s, but at least then they weren't sending their men and boys, not to mention a few women, off to war. She blinked away the threat of tears; she didn't want to ruin her mascara.

As she rounded the sidewalk on the way to the town hall, Ralph appeared in front of the school. He saluted her from the brim of his hat. "Good evening, Mayor."

Why had God taken a good man like Howard, who left behind a wife and family, and left a single man like Ralph? A lot of the time, God didn't make sense.

Chapter 2

"Mr. Quincy," Clarinda said.

Ralph smiled at such formality between two old friends, but then, he had addressed her as *Mayor*. At council meetings, they kept things on a strictly business basis.

"How are things going at the school?" Clarinda asked. "Are any more boys talking about leaving school early to enlist?"

"Not as many." Last spring, Ralph had agonized with Clarinda about two boys who had left before graduation and jumped into the fight. "I have some ideas about how to step up the war effort here at home." He rubbed his forehead. "Maybe if they feel like they're making a difference while they're still in school, they won't rush to join the army before their time."

"I look forward to hearing your ideas."

They entered the building and headed for the conference room. The council secretary, Hazel Eddy, walked around the table, placing a copy of the agenda in front of each chair. Coffee percolated in the corner, and ashtrays were set in front of a couple of seats. Clarinda's nose wrinkled. Her dislike of smoking was well-known, but she couldn't outlaw it in a public building.

Ralph flicked a glance at the agenda and smiled. "I see you left us with plenty of time for discussion about the school charter."

Her nose lifted a little higher. "All in due time, Mr. Quincy."

He hid a grin. The noise of cars pulling up in the parking lot alerted them to the arrival of the rest of the council: Ralph's friend and chief supporter, Rich Adams; Earl Chaffee and Paul Gates, both firmly in Clarinda's camp, which gave her an advantage in most matters brought before the council; and Louis Hack, city attorney, the most impartial member of the council. He had kept his opinion about the charter close to his chest. Tonight could prove interesting.

Clarinda, or Madam Mayor as she was called at council meetings, opened with a word of prayer before leading them in the Pledge of Allegiance adopted by congress over the summer. Next the council quickly approved the additional funds for snow removal.

The council members shifted in their seats as they approached the major business of the evening, a decision regarding the status of Maple Notch Female Seminary. As far as Ralph was concerned, the school was a sacred cow, unnecessary but untouchable. Rich shared Ralph's opinion, but Louis Hack was the key.

"The first order of New Business is the renewal of the charter of Maple Notch Female Seminary as an institution of secondary education. Given the institution's excellent reputation, I do not anticipate any problems with the renewal." Clarinda's crisp speech didn't indicate any worries with the process.

Liar. Ralph admired the mayor's moxie.

"Will someone make the motion for the renewal of the charter?"

"So moved," Earl said.

"Seconded," Paul said.

"Is there a need for discussion before we bring the matter to a vote?" Clarinda spoke in her brightest tone.

Ralph leaned forward. "Madam Mayor, I would like the floor."

Her smile didn't falter. "Go ahead, Mr. Quincy."

"There is absolutely no question of the importance of the seminary to Maple Notch in the past. We have all benefited from Clara Farley Tuttle's vision of providing education for the distaff half of our population and for championing women's suffrage throughout her life before proudly casting her first ballot in 1920."

He continued with a list of many of the seminary's illustrious alumnae, who had spearheaded educational, medical and political advances across the Northeast as well as going abroad as missionaries. By naming all the highlights Clarinda would mention, he hoped to steal some of her thunder.

"But more than seventy-five years have passed since the seminary opened its doors. The school has seen declining numbers for the past quarter century, to the point that there are nearly as many teachers as students."

Clarinda squirmed. He hated hurting her, but he couldn't let personal feelings interfere.

"At the same time, the quality of education at public institutions has improved dramatically for both men and women. The University of Vermont opened admission to women just a few years after the seminary was founded.

Last year, seventy-five percent of the female graduates from the Maple Notch High School went on to UVM or other institutions of higher learning."

Department by department, he listed the gains the public school, *his* school, had made as he handed out a sheet comparing the seminary to the high school in several vital categories.

"I believe our town and our country will be better served by consolidating our educational efforts to prepare our young people for the future."

Silence reigned for a few seconds before Clarinda cleared her throat. "Thank you, Mr. Quincy. Does anyone else want to add anything to his remarks?"

Earl Chaffee followed, presenting material Clarinda had probably prepared. He lacked her verve, however. Since Ralph had already made many of the same points, the information offered no counterpunch. The correct decision should be obvious to anyone with an open mind. He flicked a glance at Rich.

A chair pushed back, and Louis Hack raised his hand. "I have not come to a definite decision on this matter. I need time to consider further before making my choice." He pushed his glasses up his nose. "I confess I awaited the outcome of the election, believing this decision would be best made by the leaders the town chose for next year. Now that we know we will continue as the council is assembled, it is a different matter."

The council voted to table the discussion.

Clarinda took a sip of coffee to buy herself a second to think. "Very well. We will reconsider the question at our next meeting, in two weeks." She hated postponing the vote, but she wouldn't give Ralph the satisfaction of knowing how badly he had shaken her. "We must make a decision before the end of the year."

"Two weeks should give me ample time," Louis said.

With that behind her, Clarinda continued with the rest of the agenda. "The floor is open for New Business. Does anyone else have another matter to bring before the council this evening?"

Ralph pushed his chair back and stood. "I do, Madam Mayor." He passed around a government-issued pamphlet. "We have various ways we can contribute to the war effort, and we already have many excellent ideas in the works. But this pamphlet—" he held one up with his right hand "—explains a way we can actively engage in the war effort. The United States needs people to keep their eyes on the skies for enemy airplanes. They're called 'plane spotters.'"

The pamphlet featured a pretty young blonde holding binoculars trained on the sky. She held a notebook on her lap, her pen poised, ready to make a note of any planes. The image resembled Betty, and Clarinda shuddered.

"…the need is immediate."

Ralph paused, and Clarinda spoke into the brief silence. "We need a motion before the council to discuss the matter."

"I move that the town of Maple Notch begin a plane-spotter program," Rich Adams chimed in.

"Second." Louis Hack didn't hesitate in his support of the motion.

Every member of the council was eager to do what he or she could in the war effort and not simply send others to fight. All of them, save Ralph, had at least one son in the military. The town even had women serving, including Dr. Landrum's youngest daughter. Grandmother Clara would be proud.

Clarinda asked crisply, "What is involved? Expenses? Personnel? Training? Do you have answers to the five Ws?"

"Madam Mayor, I recommend we form a committee of two to look into the logistics for beginning such a program," Earl said. "I recommend that Mr. Quincy and I work together and bring a cohesive plan to next month's council meeting."

"All agreed, raise your right hand," Clarinda said.

As expected, that suggestion brought a unanimous vote, and Clarinda noted it on her agenda. "Very well. We will consider both of tonight's items under Old Business in two weeks' time. Meeting adjourned."

Like the old-fashioned gentleman he was, Ralph reached the coatrack first and held her coat for her. "You seemed a little unsettled by the plane-spotter program." He spoke in a low voice, so that the others couldn't overhear.

The man was too perceptive. She shook her head. "All in all, I am sure it is an excellent suggestion, provided it is run properly."

He chuckled. "This is me, Clarinda. You don't have to get all stuffy with me."

"I most certainly must be precise with you. You excel at using my very words against me." She smiled as she said it. Ralph had eased her early days as mayor. That was, until their differences of opinion became evident. "I have not had time to consider the proposal. I will not speak out of turn." Her role as mayor differed from the more familiar role of mother, as Betty liked to remind her. "Is there anything else? I promised the girls I would get home early if I could."

Disappointment flashed in his eyes as they walked down the front steps together. "I would offer you a ride home, but I know you prefer to walk." He tipped his hat and climbed into his car. "I will see you at church on Sunday."

"Until then." The temperature had dropped during the meeting and was now cold enough to cut her throat. Next time perhaps she should accept Ralph's offer of a ride, although it made no sense when the seminary was only across the town square. Walking had become a way of life with cost-cutting measures during the Depression and gas rationing during the war.

After a brisk walk across the square, Clarinda arrived at the school, and Mademoiselle DePaul, the seminary's faithful French teacher for the past twenty years, came into the hall as Clarinda entered. "Oh, Madam Finch, I am so glad you are home. Mademoiselle Tuttle is sick. Dr. Landrum is with her, and they wish to speak with you."

Aunt Flo was sick enough to call the doctor? Clarinda climbed the stairs in trepidation. Dr. Landrum sat beside her aunt's bed, the two of them deep in conversation.

"You called for me?" Clarinda took a chair on the other side of Aunt Flo's bed. Without her usual cosmetics, she looked frail, her skin the color of fragile parchment. "What's wrong?"

Aunt Flo clasped Clarinda's hand, her grasp as firm as ever. "Dr. Landrum…" She looked at the doctor, a lifelong friend, as if seeking his strength. He nodded, and she looked back at Clarinda. "He says it is time for me to step down as headmistress of the seminary. In fact—" she patted the doctor's hand as she said this "—he told me I should have retired quite some time ago. But the war started, Howard died, you stepped in as mayor, then you ran for reelection…. There wasn't a good time to turn over the reins."

"But now I insist she stop." Dr. Landrum gave Clarinda as stern a look as Aunt Flo had ever directed at a recalcitrant pupil. "I cannot speak for her health if she persists in taxing herself to her own detriment."

Don't panic. Clarinda repeated the same advice she had given herself all year. "Is there something special I should know about?"

"Mademoiselle DePaul can handle the administrative duties for a short time. I have always expected *you* to take over for me someday, but for now, you have the more important job of seeing our community through this war. I have assembled a list of possible headmistresses in my desk downstairs." Aunt Flo continued ticking off a list of instructions. This day hadn't caught her by surprise.

"I wish you had told me." The words came out without conscious thought. "If I had known, I wouldn't have run for mayor. Earl Chaffee would make a fine mayor, or even Ralph Quincy, although we disagree on a lot of issues."

"That is exactly why I did not speak up before." Aunt Flo lifted her head from the pillow. "That man wants to close our school." She patted Clarinda's hand. "I kept meaning to discuss it with you. I have some ideas that might surprise you."

"That's enough for now," Dr. Landrum interrupted. "Clarinda, I am depending on you to keep Flo from ruling the roost from her bed, the way she would like to."

"Of course." Clarinda nodded.

Change was in the air, and she didn't like it.

First bell rang. Ralph stood at the window, smiling as latecomers dashed through the doors in an effort to reach their homerooms before the final bell. Friday always saw a few students arrive a few minutes late, and even more leave a few minutes early, eager for the weekend to arrive.

Ivy Mcrriott knocked on his half-open door, waving a stack of messages, and Ralph thumbed through them. Earl

Chaffee had already called about setting up a time for their committee meeting. *Good.* Two or three slips down in the pile, he saw one from "M. Finch," with a phone number Ralph recognized as belonging to the seminary. What did Clarinda want with him this morning?

Dialing the number, he waited for the response.

"Maple Notch Female Seminary. How may I help you?"

Not Clarinda's voice. "May I speak with Mrs. Finch, please?"

No clicking of phone lines came. Instead, the voice asked, "Is this Mr. Quincy?"

"Yes."

"Oh, good. Thank you for calling back so soon. This is Betty Finch. Can you hold a minute?"

"Of course." He heard footsteps crossing the floor and a door shut. Betty came back on the line. "I should have a minute before someone comes in. Aunt Flo is sick and everything has gone crazy around here. May I come by to see you at lunchtime today? I don't have any classes, so don't worry—I'm not cutting school."

Ralph picked up a pen to make a note. "I have time, but may I ask what you wish to see me about?"

"Oh, it's all tied up with Mom and Aunt Flo and everything. I'll tell you when I get there. Someone's coming in." Ralph heard the door open. "Thank you for calling. Have a good day." Betty used her best receptionist's voice before she hung up the phone.

Hmm, what did Clarinda's daughter want to see him about? Ralph reminded himself to treat Betty as an individual and not as a member of the extensive Tuttle/Finch clan.

Later that morning, Ralph ushered one of his problem students out of the office. If Ralph could keep him in school until graduation, the army would be the perfect place for him. Checking his watch, Ralph decided he had time for his sack lunch, a bologna sandwich and an apple. He had just thrown the core in the trash can when Ivy knocked on the door.

"Come in."

"Miss Finch is here to see you." Through the open door, Betty waved at him.

"Please send her in." As Betty took her seat, Ralph considered the girl. He suspected her serious side brought her to his office today. "How can I help you, Miss Finch?"

Laying her hands on his desk, she leaned forward. "Mr. Quincy, you have to help us save the seminary."

Chapter 3

Ralph wrote down a few words while his mind sorted through the implications of what Betty had said. The gleam in her eyes suggested courage but no subterfuge. He decided to speak the plain truth. The shining intelligence in her eyes wouldn't accept anything less.

"As much as I admire everything the seminary has meant to the town of Maple Notch, I am certain you know my stance on renewing its charter. I'm against it."

Betty waved her hand as if unconcerned. "Of course I know that. I haven't told Mom this, but I agree with you. But I have a special request." She lifted her chin, an imitation of her mother's typical pose, if she but knew it. "It is important that the school close in a manner that honors its history, with dignity and purpose. Not for Mom or my family—at least, not only for us." She flashed a smile at the inclusion of herself in her plea. "But for the town and what the school represents."

As much as Ralph liked the idea, he didn't see how to

accomplish it. Without a renewed charter, the school would close when the clock struck midnight on New Year's Eve. "There's not much time."

"I know. I was going to talk with Mom about it when Arthur comes home again next week, for Thanksgiving. I know he agrees with me. But Aunt Flo is sick, and Dr. Landrum said someone else needs to take over immediately."

Poor Clarinda. "I still don't see how this affects me."

"Mademoiselle DePaul is acting as administrator for now, as well as teaching French, art and history, but she needs to drop a couple of classes if she's going to run the school. I heard her talking with Mom about it." Betty folded her hands in her lap and smiled at Ralph, her face a pretty pink. "I would like *you* to teach one or two of the history classes, at night, or after school lets out, until Christmas break. Then we could finish strong. There aren't a lot of girls enrolled, and there will be even fewer next semester." Now her face turned even redder. "I had already decided to attend the public high school next semester, but I haven't told Mom yet.

"The seminary is holding its annual Founder's Day banquet next month," she went on. "A lot of alumnae will attend, more than usual. It's the perfect time to announce the school's closure, make the event both a celebration—and a goodbye. It would be great if you and some of the other town leaders came, as well, to brag on the seminary."

Ralph settled in his chair. Betty's plan just might work. "Does your mother know you're speaking to me?"

"I think I mentioned I was coming over here today." Betty looked evasive.

So Clarinda didn't know. "There's a problem with your plan. You can't hire me as a teacher."

"I know that." Betty sounded offended. "But I thought

you could come by. Say you heard about Aunt Flo's illness, and offer to teach a class or two. It would be like an olive branch, you see, and would help Mom to feel better about things."

The girl had thought things through.

"I will ask. And we'll take it from there."

Three days later, Ralph stood at the front of an almost empty classroom, equipped with every tool a teacher might want. Someone—the students? The teachers?—had put time into creating large-scale maps of both the European and Pacific fronts, with dates and outcomes of battles noted. It represented a class on current events at its finest.

This afternoon Ralph would teach American history. Since the class of five consisted of a mixture of juniors and seniors, Betty was among the students.

To Ralph's surprise, Clarinda had fallen upon his offer to teach with alacrity. The few nerves fluttering in his stomach disappeared as the girls accepted his presence with a minimum of fuss. Before he knew it, the hour had flown by, and he taught a second class, to a group of seventh-to-ninth graders, on Vermont state history. By the end of the day, he discovered he had thoroughly enjoyed himself. Too much time had passed since he had taught in the classroom.

Clarinda's middle daughter, Norma, was in the second class. She resembled her mother more than Betty did; a serious girl, passionate about learning, perhaps destined for the teaching profession like her mother and great-grandmother before her. As she walked out, she said, "Hi, Mom," as Clarinda appeared in the doorway.

"You're a good teacher." Her smile held a little bit of sadness. "It's too bad it took Aunt Flo's illness for me to realize that. Perhaps we should rethink our position on male teachers."

He walked over to the diorama the students had created. "I, also, have learned some interesting things today. The history teachers at my school would give anything for facilities like this. Your students are as intelligent and as well mannered as I have come to expect."

Clarinda hesitated at the door before entering, as though he was the host. He said, "Come on in and take a load off. You look like you could use a friend about now."

"Thanks." A sad smile crossed her face as she took the seat. "You're right. I never realized how alone being the mayor would make me…or running the school. I've gone from being everyone's peer to their leader. And I'm not sure I like it."

Clarinda rarely showed this vulnerable side. When she handled Howard's death with such strength and grace, some people had called her "the iron lady." For her to drop her defenses showed how distraught she was—or how much she trusted him—in spite of their differences of opinion. In either case, he had been given a special privilege. "How is Miss Tuttle's health?"

Clarinda's shoulders slumped, and new lines had formed around her eyes since the beginning of the year. "Not good, not good at all. Dr. Landrum thinks she could have a stroke or a heart attack at any time." Her voice trailed off. "I've read accounts of how one of my ancestors nursed her future father-in-law through a stroke. I wonder if I'll do as well, if the need arises." She looked out the window, where the sky shaded darker and darker.

"Don't worry. You're a strong woman, Clarinda. It's one of the things I've always admired about you."

Ralph admired her? Clarinda didn't know how the conversation had turned in this direction. Ralph was a good listener. Watching him lead the class had shown that. When the girls answered his questions, he had paid close attention, sparking a lively discussion on the two-party system. Although he had used the recent local election as an example, he didn't favor either party in his teaching.

Too bad he wasn't married. He would listen to his wife, treat her as his equal, his partner, his helpmate. She had loved Howard with all of her heart, but at times…he wanted the final say.

Enough foolish thinking. She shook her head as she stood. "Thank you again for taking on the classes. I know you've put in a long day—"

"As have you." He walked with her to the door.

"I look forward to seeing you again." They said goodbye at the front door. From the window, she watched him drive away. If only he saw the future of the seminary the same way she did, instead of fighting her about it. Maybe teaching here would change his mind.

Clarinda had always confided in Aunt Flo, but now she didn't dare share the burdens with her aunt. Until she hired Aunt Flo's replacement, she was stuck at the school. Another area of concern was the extra work the staff carried. Every one of them had taught for at least twenty years, some of them as many as forty. As Marie DePaul said, "I am not getting any younger. I could do these things before, but now…" If only all their problems could be solved as simply as having Ralph take over classes for a week or two.

At the moment Clarinda wished she could head upstairs and supervise Anita's homework. Of all her children, Clarinda worried the most about her youngest. She hadn't had time to give Anita proper attention since she had lost her father. But tonight Clarinda needed to comb the office files for additional candidates for Aunt Flo's position. She stared at her notes from her last conversation with a woman she thought would be eager to consider the job. Two words summed up everything she had said: *not interested.* Her reasons troubled Clarinda greatly.

Frankly, I hope to secure a position in a school with a larger enrollment. I do not envy the task you face, finding another headmistress and increasing enrollment. Perhaps Mr. Quincy is right, Mrs. Finch. Enrollment is down. Our young women are excelling in other fields, finding other opportunities to prove their equality, and the war effort is everyone's primary concern. Perhaps it is time to consider closing the school.

The very thought made Clarinda's head hurt. Rubbing her temples didn't ease the tension. All her life, she had turned to her aunt and her husband for counsel. Now Howard was gone and her aunt, incapacitated. Ironically the person she felt most comfortable discussing thorny issues with was the one man most determined to shut down the seminary permanently.

She would use all her resources to track down candidates for the school and discuss the situation with the family over Thanksgiving. Perhaps they could help her thrash out a solution.

"Mom?" Anita bounced into the office. "Are you still working? I need help with my math homework."

With a final look at the folders on her desk, Clarinda stood with a welcome smile. "No, it's time I call it a night. Let's get that homework done and then catch up with Nancy Drew's adventures."

On Thanksgiving morning, Clarinda's sister-in-law Mary Anne shooed her out of the kitchen. "You take care of us all the time. Go, relax. Spend time with that son of yours." Mary Anne had changed a great deal from the flapper who had been stranded in Maple Notch after a car accident and ended up marrying Clarinda's brother, Wallace.

Although Arthur attended school just a short distance away at the University of Vermont in Burlington, he had come home only once this semester. Clarinda found him in the library, sitting in the chair his father used to favor in the evenings. She missed her two sons more than she cared to admit. Arthur was thumbing through a new book. At least she assumed it was new, since he had removed the jacket, the way she had taught him to do, and she inhaled the fresh paper smell.

Arthur smiled as she came in. "Macy's isn't having their usual parade today. They say they needed to conserve rubber and helium for the war effort. The Detroit Lions won't be playing today, either, of course." He shut the book and stood. "To hear the little ones, Thanksgiving without parades and football is as bad as Christmas without Santa Claus. To think of the sacrifices we have to make because of the war."

Clarinda frowned at the mocking tone. "Our family has already sacrificed."

Chagrin crossed Arthur's face. "I know, Mom." He hugged her. "But they don't seem to appreciate how good they have it."

She nodded. Howie and Arthur were old enough to have felt the pinch of the Depression.

"Then let's play a game of Parcheesi."

Clarinda wanted to put off a discussion about the seminary. Most of the women of the family stayed busy in the kitchen, but as Clarinda had suggested, they took out two Parcheesi boards and played a tournament with four teams. The winners of the first game played a second round.

Shortly after noon, Betty rang the bell and they gathered in the formal dining room. These days, the family gatherings took more seats than staff and students at the seminary. Clarinda stared at the end of the table where only last year Howard had sat, before Japan had attacked Pearl Harbor and turned their world upside down. Her brother, Wallace, stood beside her. "Do you want me to sit at the head of the table? Or Arthur?"

Neither. Clarinda's eyes filled, but she spoke with a clear voice. "You take the place, Wallace. You are the oldest male present."

As little as she wanted to bring up business during their family meal, she knew everyone would scatter at the end of the meal to clean, nap or play football. As they began their slices of pie—squash, chocolate meringue, mincemeat and apple; all good New England staples—she brought up the subject.

"We as a family need to make a decision about the future of the seminary. I have had no success in finding a headmistress for the school." She looked down the side of the table, to where Aunt Flo sat, her chin nodding. "Mary Anne, perhaps you could help Aunt Flo to bed."

"Come on, let's go lie down," Mary Anne said softly.

Aunt Flo's eyes flew open. "Let me say my piece, and I'll go." She looked straight at Clarinda as she spoke. "I have lived and breathed the Maple Notch Female Seminary for most of my life. But the time does arrive for all good things to come to an end." With a firm nod of her head, she stood and walked out with her back straight.

No one spoke into the stunned silence for long seconds. At last Wallace spoke. "What do the other trustees say, Clarinda?"

She looked at her hands before bringing her gaze back to the people around the table. "They are very concerned about the enrollment, the costs of continuing, money that perhaps should go to the war effort…the fact that our staff is reaching retirement age in the near future."

Heads around the table nodded as she mentioned each

point, but Clarinda couldn't bring herself to state the obvious conclusion. She stared at the painting of her grandmother hanging on the wall. What would Grandma do? Would she continue to push for education or pursue new opportunities for women?

Halfway down the table, Betty and Arthur exchanged looks. He nodded, and she stood. "I have an announcement to make."

Clarinda looked at her daughter, wondering what she wanted to say, but she wouldn't deny her the right to speak. "Go ahead, Betty."

"I want you to know that whether or not Maple Notch Female Seminary is open after Christmas, I'm not going back. I have already enrolled in classes at the public high school for the spring semester."

A single clap exploded in the silence, coming from Arthur. He stood as Betty sat down. "While we are making announcements, I have one of my own. I will complete the fall semester, so I earn all of my credits, but then I am enlisting in the navy. I have it all set up with the recruiting office in Burlington."

He walked around the table and helped Betty from her seat. Together they approached Clarinda. "I'll be headed for basic training the day after Christmas."

Chapter 4

Ralph enjoyed the break in the school days almost more than the students did, especially when he got to extend his hiatus by attending a three-day training session for leaders of local plane spotters. Maple Notch hadn't yet approved the program, but he believed it was just a matter of time. He had spent the week in Burlington, with other community leaders, young and old, male and female, all memorizing the provided material. Because of the number of new planes, any leader would have to stay on top of the constant changes—a challenging job.

Before he began on the day's studies, however, he called his secretary to check on the school. "Anything new happening up in Maple Notch? All our boys still accounted for?" The time spent studying enemy planes, weapons and insignia had sharpened rather than relieved his fears. The more he learned, the more he became convinced that this would be a prolonged, lengthy battle for freedom, even worse than the Great War.

Reveille called, as it did in the military, the training for spotters as disciplined and serious as any he had received before being shipped to Flanders.

He raced down the stairs—always a race to see who would get to be first in line—until he met up with Emma Beacham. The oldest of their group but perhaps the sharpest, Emma descended the stairs at a steady pace. He slowed to match her steps. "I don't know why I catapult myself down the stairs like that. I'm as bad as the boys at my school, eager to be first."

"Boys can be like that." She nodded. Ralph didn't know much about Emma, beyond the fact she was another Maple Notch Female Seminary graduate leading the war effort. Sandwiched between Flo and Clarinda in age, he'd guess, a woman who had gone on to study the law and serve the people of her community as a state representative for several years before her recent retirement.

"You're from Maple Notch, didn't you say?" Emma asked.

She phrased it as a question, but Ralph was sure she knew the answer. "I'm the principal of the high school."

"Ah. That puts you directly in Clarinda Finch's crosshairs."

Ralph smiled in agreement. That phrased it well.

"What is this I've heard about the school closing?"

Ralph held his breath. "Nothing is certain."

"I am sorry to see the seminary close its doors, but I fear its end has come. Is she going to close the school in time to help lead your community into fully supporting the war effort, or is she still trying to pull the dinosaur along with her?"

Ralph wasn't quite sure how to respond. He agreed with

her sentiments, but to speak of it felt like betraying Clarinda. "I've seen signs that she is coming around. I am interested in your opinion, as one of the seminary's illustrious graduates."

Emma smiled at his compliment. "I am speaking with other graduates, to encourage Mrs. Finch to make the move. If she knows that we who respect the school and its traditions feel the time to close has come, perhaps the transition will be easier. She is such a powerful presence. I hate to see her bogged down when her strength could make such a difference elsewhere."

"I couldn't agree with you more. I think that's an excellent idea."

They turned the corner leading to the mess hall. Tom Gaines, the instructor, handed out slim blue boxes as they entered. After they finished eating, he sent a double deck of cards around the table, inviting the students to take up the games of canasta, which had been played almost nonstop since their arrival. "With all the slides and movies and pamphlets available, who would ever have expected that the most effective educational tool for this discipline would be a pack of cards?" He shook his head. Different members of the axis represented the four suits, and each numbered card showed a different model plane. Instead of waiting for the card to appear in the deck, they had to identify the plane on the card and ask for it by name one time. Next by the number of wings; other times, the colors, engines, special markings, even sounds.

Ralph came out the winner this morning. His knack for telling one car from another had served him well today, transferring readily to his identification of different aircraft. He lifted his hands in triumph, pulling all the cards toward him, as if he had all the munitions available in the war. If only it were that simple.

"So what are the boxes about?" Jim, a wheelchair-bound banker, asked.

"Since this is our last day, I wanted to give you something as a token for all your hard work and as another suggestion to use with your local groups. You earned these as soon as you could name every plane."

Ralph laughed when he opened the box to find a yellow silk tie, decorated with different enemy aircrafts. The ladies received a scarf made out of a similar material. Nestled in the box next to the tie was a tie clasp, or a bolo for the women, with the insignia for the Civilian Plane Spotter Program that the government of Vermont had instituted.

After his final pep talk, Tom bade them farewell. "We were unprepared when the Japanese slipped up on us at Pearl Harbor, but that won't happen again. No, sir, not as long as we have plane spotters to keep an eye on our skies. The first threat came from the West, but here in New England, we are only a short dash across the Atlantic from northern Europe, where Hitler has established a stronghold in Scandinavia. Our work is urgent. We are indeed on the front lines of the defense of all we hold most dear."

Ralph was ready to get home, back to work, at school and at defense, and wind up the semester for the Maple Notch seminarians. Emma stopped him as he walked past her. "I will get in touch with you, before we have the banquet," she said. "I can count on your help with Mrs. Finch, can I not?"

Anything, anytime. If only Clarinda could see him as someone other than an adversary.

Clarinda rubbed her temples. Her eyes were bone-dry, her head pounded, and she didn't know when she would get a good night's sleep again. She didn't know if it was possible, not here in the dormitory, where it seemed every trip to the powder room was accompanied by a century's worth of creaks in the floorboards. No matter what hour of the day or night she took a shower, the water was never warm enough. She shook herself. Her foul mood had nothing to do with noises or water temperature or anything.

She couldn't stop thinking about Arthur, who had decided to leave school. *Leave school!* Not even Howard had done that during the Great War. No mother, no wife, should have to face losing her husband and sons in war.

She would not cry in here, not where she might wake up Anita. No need to worry a ten-year-old with her own pain. Instead, she slipped into a silk robe and terry slippers. Experience told her life didn't come in neat packages. Look at everything Wallace and Mary Anne had been through, protecting Mary Anne from the mob and gin runners, back when she'd first arrived in Maple Notch. Or look at her sister, Winnie, and her husband, Frank, and everything they had gone through to accomplish her dream of a figure-skating championship.

But had Grandma Clara had to fight her family as well as parents and her own students? Her hero had come home from the war, and her sons had been too old for Cuba.

God had planned for Clarinda to be born in one century and grow up in the next, along with all the changes that had come along with the years. Cars replaced horses and right on their heels came machines that could fly.

She put on her coat and slipped out onto the lawns. Dew that would turn into frost by morning dampened the soles of her slippers, but the temperature wasn't too cold. She took a seat on the swing and started a gentle rocking motion.

The swing was her favorite part of the Bailey Mansion. The only swing they had at the farm was a tire swing that the children used.

So Betty wanted to graduate from the public high school. Howard would never have agreed. Of course, he had opposed Winnie's competing in ice skating at the international level all those years ago. Winnie had pursued her dream in spite of his opposition, and look at how well it had turned out. God would direct Betty's path, as well, even if it took a different turning than her mother and grandmother's.

Clarinda turned her face to the sky. If only she could read Betty's future in the stars, but God said He engraved His will on her heart. Tonight the stars scattered around the sky like needle pricks in a curtain, allowing all the known constellations and a few more fanciful ones to take form. There was the North Star, the guiding light for slaves seeking freedom in Canada. Not many had found their way through Vermont, but she would bet Grandma Clara would have taken part.

Grandma Clara had fought a different war in a different time. She was a bright, shining star for women after the Civil War, but would she say Clarinda was holding women back from taking the next step by clinging to the past?

If God's voice was whispering in her ear, Clarinda couldn't tell for all the confusion competing for her attention, but stargazing helped her focus. She began counting with the farthest star she could see to her left. Its light flickered less than the others. What did scientists say? That by the time the light of a dying star reached Earth, the star had already died.

When Clarinda had counted the stars in an inch of sky, she had relaxed enough to quit. *God is light, and in him is no darkness at all. The city had no need of the sun, for the Lamb is the light thereof.* The same God who created all those countless stars guided her today. That out of the thousands, billions, of stars, He called her by name and knew how many hairs were on her head. As heavily as her present problems weighed on her, they weren't even a teardrop in the oceans of time.

Ralph had taught history, and knew more about its ebb and flow than Clarinda did. He would listen to her current dilemmas with a good perspective, if she dared to ask.

Ralph returned to Maple Notch late that evening, after ordering supplies for training, except for binoculars. Any expensive equipment beyond the one set he received in training could wait until Maple Notch approved the program, but he had found a reliable supplier for them, as well.

The mandatory blackout couldn't keep the stars from shining, and driving was easy under the quarter moon. Before he knew it, he had reached the bridge connecting east and west Maple Notch. He pulled his car to the side of the road and trained his binoculars on the sky. Instantly the black-tipped wings of a chickadee came into view.

Where would they locate a tower for the plane spotters? The church's bell tower? A radio tower? Too far away. A shack above the covered bridge? Someone with a better head for heights and angles could figure that out.

After he got behind the wheel again, he snaked his way across the bridge, the wheels gripping the deck, rumbling loud enough for anyone within a mile to hear. Snow drifted down, faster and faster, until he had to turn on the windshield wipers. The car skidded to the right. He eased off the speed by yet another few ticks.

A few minutes later, he spotted a figure in front of the seminary as he drove around the town square. What was Clarinda doing outside in the middle of the night? As he parked, he saw a snow shovel in her hands.

He got out of the car and approached her. "Let me do that," he said, taking the shovel out of her hands.

"It's no trouble, really."

"Let someone help you for once." Ralph knew he was snapping, but this proud woman wouldn't let anyone help her if she could find a way around it.

She paused but said, "All right. At least let me fix you a hot cup of tea when you're finished."

"Sounds good." In his opinion, not enough snow had accumulated to make shoveling necessary. Something other than snow had called Clarinda outdoors in this inclement weather.

Five minutes later she welcomed him into the front parlor. "I made us tea, unless you would prefer coffee? I know some men think tea is a lady's beverage, although I've always found it to be a bracing drink myself."

"Tea is fine." In another time, a plate of cookies would have joined the teapot on the tray, he suspected, but these days everything was rationed. President Roosevelt had promised freedom from want in his last inaugural address, and anyone who had lived through the Depression and this war could appreciate the fierce desire for that so-called "freedom."

"Would you like to hear what I learned at the plane-spotter training?" Ralph asked.

"Of course." Clarinda's eyes tightened as he showed her the playing cards and explained the minute differences distinguishing one from another. "They believe the threat is very real. It's a much closer hop for Germany to cross the Atlantic than the Japanese managed at Pearl Harbor."

Clarinda nodded. "Pearl Harbor. It's been a year, next Monday." She set down her cup and walked to the front of the fireplace, where she had started a small fire to warm the room.

"I know I must make a decision about the school." Clarinda stiffened as she said the words. "I promise you this. I will make a final determination by next Monday."

Chapter 5

"**R**alph, please open our meeting tonight with a word of prayer." Whatever differences lay between Clarinda and Ralph, she was certain he had spent as much time discussing the situation with God as she had. Tonight the town council would decide the future of Maple Notch Female Seminary.

After the amen, Hazel passed out the agenda. In addition to the two tabled items from the last meeting, Clarinda had added a third item, which had been brought to her attention by the state of Vermont. Because of the new factory south of town, traffic across the Bumblebee River had increased, creating the need for a new bridge.

"The first order of business tonight is the question of the renewal of the charter for Maple Notch Female Seminary." Clarinda spoke the words with the same clarity and crispness as any other issue coming before the council. She had her usual veiled hat on, which she hoped hid the thoughts and emotions running through her mind.

Louis Hack cleared his throat. "If my understanding of the question is clear, the charter determines whether students attending the seminary will receive academic credentials equal to those attending a public school of learning. Is this correct?"

Of course it was. Clarinda and Ralph nodded in unison.

"Then the question before the council reduces to a simple matter. Does the seminary, in spite of the many changes Mr. Quincy so eloquently pointed out at the last council meeting, continue to meet the academic standards as demanded by the state of Vermont and as stipulated in our town's laws?"

Louis had captured the issue with such simplicity. "I checked the record of recent graduates of the seminary, as well as the pending plans for the girls expecting to graduate next May. They all have been accepted to the colleges of their choice, and many also desire more active involvement in the war effort."

Clarinda caught Ralph in a short shake of his head.

"My point is, the graduates meet or exceed state standards," Louis said. "Therefore, it is my considered opinion that the school charter must remain in place."

Clarinda didn't move, not quite believing Louis's support. After the last meeting, she had felt sure the decision would go against her. Now Louis had handed it to her on a platter.

Ralph stared straight ahead, his gaze fixed on a world map that Clarinda used to track the battles both in Europe and the Pacific. His supporter, Rich, stared at his hands. No one else spoke.

"Does anyone have anything further to say on the subject?" Clarinda held her breath.

"Call the question," Earl Chaffee said.

"Everyone in favor of renewing the charter of the Maple Notch Female Seminary, please lift your right hand," Clarinda said.

Three hands went up immediately, but before Clarinda could ask for the votes against, Rich's hand slowly went up, then shot back down. Four votes in favor. The seminary's continuance was legally ratified.

"Everyone against renewing the charter of the Maple Notch Female Seminary, please signify by lifting your right hand." Clarinda waited for Ralph to raise his hand.

Instead, he kept the palms of both hands flattened against the table, the pointer finger of his left hand tattooing an inaudible beat.

"Let the record reflect that the charter for Maple Notch Female Seminary has been renewed by a vote of four in favor and one abstention."

"Madam Mayor, if I may address the council?" Louis asked.

"Go ahead," said Clarinda.

All lean six feet of Louis stood to address the others. "I found no reason to vote against renewing Maple Notch's charter due to academic performance. However, for all the reasons Mr. Quincy so eloquently outlined at our last meeting, I agree that the time has come for the venerable institution to close its doors before it becomes a shadow of its former self. I'm getting out of the realm of governing and into meddling, but as a member of this community who has benefited from the presence of the seminary in our midst, I must speak my mind."

"Very well. Does anyone else have something to say?" Clarinda took a sip of water to combat the sudden dryness in her throat.

Ralph shook his head. "Except to agree. I wish to see

the seminary close its doors on a high note, a dignified ending to a historic institution. But as Mr. Hack has said, that takes me from governing to meddling." He paused. "Are we ready to address the question of the plane-spotter program?"

"Affirmative," Clarinda said.

"Then we shall begin a game of go fish." With a grin, Ralph brought out a double deck of cards and shuffled them with several flicks of his wrist before passing them among the council members.

"Mr. Quincy," Clarinda reprimanded him.

"Have patience for a moment, Madam Mayor. My purposes will become clear." Ralph ran down his activities during the training program. "Rich, I have the address of several places where you can buy these cards, but I brought back a pack apiece for the members of the council."

The game was played the same as the familiar version of the card game, except that instead of asking for an eight of spades, the player might ask for a Messerschmitt Bf 109 fighter instead or whatever plane was on the card. The person could try to give a different card—a Dornier Do 17 bomber, say—and if the first player didn't recognize the difference, the second got to keep both cards.

The men enjoyed the game, and Clarinda saw the educational value of studying the differences between enemy aircraft. They played several hands.

"Now you have the real test." Ralph introduced the theme much the same way that their teacher had at last week's workshop, but why change what worked? "Here is a reel of film from a recent part of the battle over Britain that features planes from both sides of the conflict. Call out planes you recognize."

Ralph knew each and every one, since he had watched

it repeatedly until he could identify them within seconds. Tonight he wanted the council to have a taste of real plane spotting. Only Clarinda remained uninterested, shrugging when Ralph sent her a questioning glance.

When the film ran out of the projector, Ralph turned the lights back on and went to the plane poster he had tacked to the wall. "Well done! You correctly identified twenty-five of the aircraft."

Louis chuckled. "Out of how many?"

Ralph hesitated. "Two hundred thirty-two."

Clarinda smiled at that one. "I saw plane spotters in the film, didn't I?" she asked.

"Several on the roofs, yes. In fact, the spotters are part of the reason why those brave British aces have done so well. We will shoulder a similar responsibility here."

After that, the council listened to his plan of action. "I have a proposal for instituting a watch program immediately." His poor secretary had had quite a day of it, typing multiple copies of the proposal, but as usual, she had come through.

Clarinda slipped on her reading glasses, her lips thinning as she scanned the lines. "This is a very aggressive timetable."

"Why not?" Ralph used the smile that Rich said made women swoon, but more important, he had the facts on his side. "How would we feel if we could have prevented an enemy strike but had left preparation too late?"

The men nodded.

"With your permission, I will get an article about the program in the next newspaper, as well as bulletins at businesses and in the schools. I definitely hope to include students from the seminary in the watch program. Older youths are among the best watchers, with the sharpest eyes, clearest vision for details and ability to concentrate during the watches of the night."

"So you want our young girls to sit in an isolated location, alone, for hours in the evening? Is that…safe…Mr. Quincy?" Clarinda asked.

"For that very reason I plan to include training in small arms for all our recruits, for anyone not used to handling guns. If we have enough volunteers, we may also choose to assign two spotters at the same time. I am hoping for a good-sized group."

"I see you also recommend different spotter locations in the future." Clarinda frowned at the paper. "Who will pay for their construction?"

"I agree." Louis tapped the page with his pencil. "These numbers would put a strain on a budget just now recovering from the Depression."

"I don't believe we need to raises taxes for the program. Enthusiasm for war bonds is at an all-time high. Rich, I wondered if you would be willing to talk with the other retailers about an exchange of stamps for equipment? We need four sets minimum to begin with and can add as the program grows. What say you, Madam Mayor?" Ralph looked into Clarinda's brilliant gray-brown eyes. "It's time to call the question."

The proposal passed, but the men continued discussing details. Clarinda focused on the world map. After a brief interval, she banged her gavel. "Order, please. We still have one item on the agenda for this evening, the new bridge the state is constructing to connect the factory south of town with its customers."

The Tuttles had been instrumental in constructing the original covered bridge, as well as the bridge that crossed the Bumblebee now. How hard it must be for Clarinda, who seemed to lose ties to the past faster than they were being replaced.

"May I walk you home?" Ralph asked when the meeting broke up.

Clarinda smiled her answer. She tugged on a pair of boots, a nuisance except for the protection they offered from the slush underfoot. At least slush was safer than straight ice, which they would find in the morning, if the temperature didn't rise.

Ralph took Clarinda's arm as they maneuvered around the sidewalk. "I wonder if we ordered enough road salt for this year."

"We're thinking along the same lines."

"I notice we do that a lot." Ralph sidestepped a puddle. "We don't always agree, but we often follow the same lines of reasoning."

"Maybe that stems from having the same debate teacher in high school." Clarinda stopped moving when they reached the front of the seminary. "Do you care for a cup of coffee before you drive home?" She asked out of politeness, but Clarinda wanted nothing more than a few minutes with her girls before hitting her soft pillow. Tonight, with the pressure of the vote about the school behind her, she hoped she could rest.

"Not this evening. But perhaps…" He looked at her, then glanced away, as if uncertain how she might respond. "Perhaps I could take you out for dinner one of these days, to thank you for your support of the plane-spotter program?"

Ralph sought more and more of her attention these days. Some days she almost felt as if they were co-mayors. She tamped down the smile. She could think of worse people to lead Maple Notch through the war. "Let's plan on it, then," she said before she changed her mind.

Rather than the peace and quiet Clarinda usually encountered upon entering the house in the evening, she heard a wailing infant and an older child crying. The sounds emanated from the back rooms, where she and Anita lived. As she drew close, she realized that the sounds came from the kitchen, not her rooms. She stopped long enough to put away her purse, coat, hat and boots, and hurried down the hall.

Betty, Norma and Anita each held a child in her arms. Anita seemed the most successful, as she played pattycake with a smiling toddler. A little boy mopped milk and cookies from the floor with Norma. Betty held a baby who pushed away the bottle of milk she offered. Three other children crawled on the floor, as if seeking a way of escape.

"What is going on?" Clarinda asked.

Betty swung around, and the baby's crying increased. The panic on her daughter's face pushed Clarinda's questions aside.

"Let me see that baby."

"She's used to nursing.... I can't get her to take the bottle...."

"Let's get these children to the parlor. Then you can tell me what is going on." Clarinda pinched her nose. "No, that won't do. Anita, draw a bath for the ones able to sit on their own. I trust we have a change of clothes?" Anita nodded.

"Norma, set up beds in the parlor. I'll turn on the radio in there. I believe there is an all-night music station that may help calm them, or you can sing hymns or whatever. Music usually helps. And I'll take this one."

The baby's face scrunched in angry red lines while she continued to squall, sucking on tiny fists before renewing her cries. Clarinda took her from Betty. "Go ahead and fix a new bottle for this little one here. Not too hot, comfortable as tap water on your skin, and bring it to me in the parlor."

The girls scattered to their various assignments, and Clarinda took the infant to her favorite rocking chair in the parlor. She twisted the knobs on the radio and found the station she sought. "Blue moon, you saw me standing alone." She danced and hummed the melody, but the baby didn't quiet at all.

Ten years had passed since Anita was a baby, but raising five children had taught Clarinda a few tricks. She built up the fire so the room would be warm enough for the baby. She unwrapped the infant, determined to start from the skin out. The diaper was dry, so that wasn't the cause of her distress. "You're just missing your mother, aren't you, little one?"

Betty scampered into the parlor. "I think this is right."

Hard to believe her eldest daughter could be married and a mother herself a little more than a year from now. Given that, why did Clarinda worry about Betty's choice of school? By the time Clarinda was Betty's age, she was acting as mother to her younger brother and sister after their parents died in the flu pandemic. She had kept trying to guide her siblings' decisions for far too long. She wanted to avoid that mistake with her children. She and Betty needed to talk about public school, soon.

Right now Clarinda required an explanation for the sudden appearance of the six tots in the kitchen. She offered the bottle to the infant, who took a quick taste and began whimpering again. "Who is this?"

"She's Hattie Charles's baby. Mrs. Rucker takes care of several of these children at night, while their moms work at the factory, but tonight there was an emergency at the church, and she asked if we could step in, and I said yes and..." Betty stopped. "Please don't get mad at me. I know you wouldn't want us babysitting, but it was urgent, and you weren't here."

"You meant well, but this little lady has no interest in anyone except her mother, and she's disturbing everyone's sleep. What if something had happened before I returned?"

Betty straightened her shoulders and looked her mother straight on. "I would have dealt with the emergency." She reached for the infant. "Screaming babies don't qualify as emergencies, not unless there is something wrong. And Ruby here is fine, just missing her mother." Ruby's lips rippled but she quieted a bit. "I have an idea, if you're willing to listen."

Clarinda nodded. When had she given Betty the feeling she wouldn't listen to her? Name any occasion over the past twelve months. She sighed.

"You say to finish school, college even, before I worry about the war. But I want to help now. The children are only one example of things I can do right now. Mrs. Rucker can't take care of all the children of the factory workers by herself and certainly not for all three shifts. We could do something to help with that right here. We have plenty of space. And the plane spotting and the factory work itself." Betty sighed and flopped down in her chair. "I know school is important, but we have to win this war."

She was losing sight of the forest for the trees. Betty wouldn't appreciate a lecture on the subject.

"You should be the first to know." Clarinda stood and put her hands at the small of her back, twisting to work out the kinks from a day spent sitting. "I don't plan on making a public announcement until Monday, the anniversary of the attack on Pearl Harbor, but I have decided that you are right. Maple Notch Female Seminary will close at the end of the semester."

Chapter 6

Ralph was scanning the essays turned in for the civics class when Clarinda's shadow passed in front of the door before she entered. She stood there, almost shyly.

"Come on in. I'm just grading papers."

"Thank you again for pitching in with the classes," she said. "I'm holding a press conference in a few minutes. You'll want to attend."

He raised an eyebrow. A press conference on the anniversary of the attack on Pearl Harbor made sense, but why did she want him to come? It had to be important. He shuffled the papers into his briefcase and snapped it shut. "No time like the present, then." He followed her out the door, admiring her figure as she moved. The black-heeled boots and coat emphasizing her delicate shoulders made her appear regal and alert at the same time. She could teach some of the girls at the high school a thing or two about how to make a good impression.

He followed her down the hall toward the front parlor, where students and teachers had gathered. His suspicion grew more certain. She had reached a decision about the school.

Clarinda turned to him, an unusual degree of uncertainty written in her eyes. He patted her shoulder and smiled, and she strode forward with the confidence of a brigadier general. "In a few minutes, I will hold a press conference for the people of Maple Notch commemorating Pearl Harbor, but it is fitting that you gathered here today should hear this part of the news first."

She swallowed, and Ralph wondered if she needed a cup of water to moisten her throat. "The Maple Notch Female Seminary will close its doors at the end of this semester. Girls, I have spent today contacting your parents. I promise to make your transition to other schools as simple as possible. As far as future plans for the school…the Bailey Mansion, perhaps I should say…I am looking into the need for a boardinghouse for women working at the factory south of town."

One of the teachers broke the silence. "Bravely said, Mrs. Finch! Let us offer a round of applause for the courage to make this difficult decision."

At that a smattering of clapping broke out. Ralph took the time to study Clarinda's daughters. The middle Finch girl, Norma, looked stunned. Anita tugged at Clarinda's arm. "Does this mean I won't go to the seminary?"

Clarinda nodded but didn't speak. Tears probably hovered beneath the surface, ready to spill over if she opened her mouth again. Ralph stepped into the void. "If you continue at the Maple Notch schools, I promise we'll take good care of you."

Anita took a step closer to her mother, and Betty joined Clarinda on her other side. A glance at the older girl told

Ralph she had known the secret. She had known and probably had rejoiced—and yet here she was, supporting her mother. A good girl, well on her way to growing into a good woman.

"And now I must leave you all for town hall. You are welcome to join me, or you may choose to stay here and discuss the coming changes."

Ralph stepped forward and put himself between Clarinda and the students who threatened to mob her, her daughters falling in behind. They marched out the front door, down the sidewalk and around the square in tandem. The reporter Henshaw waited for them in front of town hall, along with the other members of the town council—Hazel must have called everyone. Rich looked at him, a question mark evident in his posture. Ralph waved him away. Now that Clarinda had made the necessary decision, Ralph had no desire to gloat over the situation.

After Clarinda took her spot behind the mike stand, Ralph joined Rich on the sidelines. "What's up?" Rich asked.

Ralph shook his head.

Clarinda began to speak. After a few thoughtful comments on the anniversary, how far the war effort had come and how far they had yet to travel—a rousing call to perseverance, patience and sacrifice—she ended with a brief mention of the closure of the seminary.

Rich narrowed his eyes at Ralph. "Why didn't you tell me?" he asked.

"I just found out myself a few minutes ago."

Rusty Henshaw stepped forward. "Do you have future plans for the Bailey Mansion, then? Will it revert to a private residence?"

"I'm glad you asked that question. It has come to my attention that several women in our community are working at the new munitions factory and are in need of housing closer to their work. We are looking into converting the Bailey Mansion into a boardinghouse."

After that, questions erupted, until Clarinda called a halt. "Our plans are only in the beginning stages. I will ask that anyone interested in living at the dormitory—we will consider both single women and mothers—to contact the mayor's office. We will accept your applications as we consider the best way to meet the needs."

Ralph broke away from the group, brushing away those who wanted to congratulate him on his "victory." Instead he headed to Clarinda. "I know this was a difficult decision for you to make. I believe with all my heart it was the right thing to do, but 'right' and 'easy' often make uneasy companions."

Clarinda shrugged, a thin veneer keeping her eyes bright and cheeks pink. "I thought you might want to gloat."

"If you thought that, you don't know me at all," Ralph whispered in Clarinda's ear. "If there is anything I can do to help with the transition, feel free to ask me."

She chuckled. "I already have a few ideas in mind. Don't worry. You may be sorry you ever volunteered."

"I doubt that." He shoved his hands into his pockets. "I'd be happy to spread the news for people needing a home, as well, while we're recruiting volunteers for plane spotters. There might be some crossover between the two groups."

"And I can return the favor, if you wish." She smiled.

Ralph wondered how much that offer cost Clarinda.

Miss Pepper, the seminary's long-suffering math professor, hovered in front of Clarinda's desk at the seminary office. "I gave Norma every opportunity to bring up her grades, but she hasn't applied herself to her studies.

I hate to bother you with this, but I'm sure you'll want to address the problem with her before she transfers to another school."

Clarinda shuffled through the math papers in front of her and checked the pages against the record book Pauline kept for each student. Norma, who entered the seminary as an honors student in English, had always found math difficult but never to this extent.

Even more disturbing than the poor grades—represented by Cs and Ds—were the zeros. On several days Norma had failed to turn in her assignment at all. "Oh, my. Every night I ask the girls if they've done their homework but haven't looked at actual assignments much lately...." Clarinda's voice trailed away. Between the school and the town, she had neglected the people who needed her the most. "That's the problem, isn't it? I haven't paid close enough attention."

"That's not for me to say, I'm sure."

"I'll talk with Norma about it," Clarinda said. "If she turns in the missing homework, can we make up her grade to a C average?"

"If the work is correct, of course, Mrs. Finch. Or I can provide more problems to solve if she needs additional practice."

Clarinda made note of the homework assignments from the pages of the textbook and bade the professor goodbye. Occasionally girls took Pauline's quiet manner for a mouse and sought to take advantage of her good disposition. They quickly discovered their error, but no one in the Tuttle family had ever been less than an ideal student. Even Winnie had performed acceptably at the seminary, in spite of her overriding interest in figure skating.

The law of averages was bound to catch up with them, but why now? Clarinda shut her eyes. She rang her bell, and Betty came in.

Betty's presence in the office also indicated the need for change. In the past, Aunt Flo had a secretary, both of them involved solely in administration. Now Clarinda taught, administered the school and led the town with only her daughter to help with the paperwork at the school.

"Do you know where Norma is?" Clarinda asked.

"At the parsonage," Betty said. "She's over there until supper, helping Mrs. Rucker with the children."

And neglecting her homework. Clarinda bit her lip to keep from losing her temper, and her mood didn't improve as she struggled into her coat and boots.

Before Clarinda could leave, Betty stopped. "Have some tea." She held out a cup.

"I need to talk with Norma about her grades."

"Have some tea first. Here, let me help you." Betty set the tea on a coaster and eased the coat from her mother's shoulders. "I even scoured up some bread and jam. You need to eat something before you rush out of here."

When had Betty become the parent? So much had changed in recent weeks. Clarinda didn't know how much more she could handle.

"I'll help Norma with her homework. I offered before, but she said no." Betty drank tea but didn't touch the bread and jam.

"You *knew?*" *And didn't tell me?*

"I think she gave up on it once they got past simple equations. I mean, I find it boring and don't see how it's going to help me. I was never so glad to finish a subject as when I finished geometry."

"You sound like me." Clarinda broke the bread into small chunks to savor each bite of the sweet jam before she swallowed the last of the tea. "You're right. The food helped." Clarinda let her fingers rest featherlight on Betty's shoulders. "Pray for me."

"Always, Mom. Always." Betty helped Clarinda back into her coat, and Clarinda headed out. Today the sun warmed the afternoon air above freezing, and the walk to the church, on the second leg of the town square, was pleasant exercise. Norma played with children outside the church, running through a pile of half-frozen leaves.

Clarinda waited a few minutes without speaking or moving, watching her middle daughter at play. She was good with children. She'd make a good teacher or a mother someday, provided she got those grades up enough to get into a good college. Math or any other subject with a D average would not look good on her transcript.

Before long, one of the children spotted Clarinda and pointed at her. Norma froze when she saw her mother.

Clarinda pasted a smile on her face. When had she ever done anything to make her daughter afraid of her?

Mrs. Rucker came outside, waving to Clarinda before calling the children inside.

"You're good with the children." Clarinda took a spot on the church's swing set.

"Thanks." Norma joined her. "They're good, most of the time."

"We need to talk." Clarinda gently rocked the swing back and forth, the toe of her boot scuffing the dry leaves underfoot. Only a few firs added color to the cold-stripped trees. "Miss Pepper came to see me today."

"Oh." Norma shifted her feet.

Norma wasn't making things easy for her mother. "I can understand poor grades when you're struggling. What distresses me is the number of incomplete and missing assignments. What's happening?"

Norma frowned at her shoes. "What difference does x equals three make when our boys are off fighting a war?"

Clarinda restrained herself from pointing out the boys

fought so their loved ones could continue with a normal life. "Equations are important to the war. Think about it. They tell pilots how far they can fly on the fuel in their tanks and at what altitude. Math also tells them what angle to shoot a target."

Norma kicked the leaves under her feet. "I suppose you would tell me math could help me figure out how many bags of leaves drop from a single tree."

Smiling, Clarinda nodded. "Here is what I'll do. Come to my office after school every day. You may babysit—"

Norma grinned.

"—*after* you bring your average back up to a C."

"If I have to." Norma stood. "Can I go now?"

Was that all it took? Clarinda shook her head. She should have been paying better attention.

Applications for plane spotters and the plans for the remodeled seminary covered the conference table in the teacher's lounge. Ralph and Clarinda had set apart the afternoon to review them. Ralph had files open for Carol Jones, Audrey Smith, Daisy Earl and Edna Dale. All four of them had graduated from the public high school. Did Clarinda have any personal knowledge of the women?

"Edna would have done well at the seminary, if she had chosen to attend." Ralph tapped the page in front of him. "But she married right after graduation and now has three little ones in need of the babysitting services on offer."

"She would need a larger room." Clarinda made a note on her legal pad. "I have opened a can of worms by offering rooms for families as well as women alone. We may have a waiting list."

"You may." Audrey Smith was a fair student, as well, but Daisy's and Carol's academic standings put them in the bottom half of their class. Of course, as he often reminded his teachers, not everyone could be star pupils, but Daisy and Carol didn't even try. Now their husbands were fighting this war. They were so young to carry such a heavy burden, younger even than he was when he fought in France in the Great War.

"I can barely read this one. I think her name is Hattie. Maybe it's Hettie. Chilton? No, it's Charles. I think." Clarinda looked up from the application. "Some of these women can barely write. I thought you said the public school produced good students." Her tone challenged him to respond.

"We do. The seminary always picked from the cream of the crop. You know that. Some students aren't capable, or their families don't care, or they just don't study. Hattie's a little slow, but she has a big heart." He peeked at the application. "Good, I'm glad she has a job at the factory. She'd do well at that, with supervision. But she would not be a good candidate for plane spotting."

"So it's less important to put together munitions than it is to spot an enemy plane?"

"That's not what I said." As so often when Ralph sat down with Clarinda, they engaged in a war of words. "When we finish going through these, perhaps we should play a word game." He wiggled his eyebrows. "I'd like to see who wins."

That comment brought surprise to Clarinda's face. "Why not? Only until dinner, of course. I want to go over Norma's math homework with her."

"Math." Ralph wrinkled his nose. "Not my favorite subject."

"Mine either, although I remember you doing well with the school math club."

Heat dashed into his cheeks. His stellar academic record looked good on his résumé when he interviewed for a job, but in general he avoided talking about it.

Clarinda leaned forward and motioned him closer. He moved closer, their faces only inches apart across the table. "Don't worry," she whispered. "In this house, it's okay to be smart."

He laughed soundly at that comment. "Thanks."

At the end of the hour, Clarinda had identified enough women and families to fill the seminary after remodeling. Ralph had two dozen solid leads for plane spotters, after he checked the references for the ones he didn't know.

Clarinda pushed her list of names across the table. "Did all these women attend high school?"

Ralph worked through the list, keeping track of their married names. "Yes, they all attended. But they didn't all graduate. Four of them left early."

"That offends my sensibilities as a teacher, and it holds them back. I wonder if they would be interested in obtaining their high school equivalency?"

"An excellent idea. In fact, I'll help."

Clarinda frowned. She wasn't going to object, was she?

"You don't have to do it all yourself, you know," Ralph said.

The tension in her shoulders eased. "I know, but I feel like I am taking advantage of you." A fleeting smile crossed her face. "And I don't want to lose a good friend."

"You don't have to worry." Ralph pushed the words out of a suddenly dry throat. "You could never take advantage of me. I want to help."

Chapter 7

Friday afternoon, the 18th of December, 1942: closing day
of the Maple Notch Female Seminary. Clarinda straightened the files the high school needed for student transfers
and then stacked the folders in her briefcase, fighting the
urge to cry. Those folders reversed Grandma Clara's decision to open a school for girls who showed promise in
academics and leadership. In spite of bowing to the inevi-
table, Clarinda wasn't ready.

Betty came in. "Is that it?" She pointed to the briefcase.

Clarinda nodded.

"I'll come with you." Betty picked up the briefcase and
slipped her arm through her mother's elbow.

"Thank you." After they put on their coats, they walked
in companionable silence around the town square and
down the road to the high school, half a block from the
town hall.

How different this school seemed, with tiled floors instead of wood and lockers lining wide hallways. Young men and women filled every classroom she glanced into. "This is the French class." Betty pointed through a window. "I'll be in her advanced class next semester. At least that's what she told me."

Clarinda nodded. What would her education have been like, if she had attended a public school? A shy girl, she sometimes felt uncomfortable around men. She had often thanked the Lord for bringing Howard into her life.

Around the corner, they arrived at the principal's office. Ralph's secretary, Ivy, stepped around her desk. "Mrs. Finch, Miss Finch, how lovely to see you. May I get you some coffee?"

Accepting the cup, Clarinda wondered if Ralph knew she had arrived.

"Mr. Quincy will be with you shortly. He has a student with him, with the parents. It's sad, really." Ivy shook her head.

Clarinda's curiosity raised its head, but she refrained from asking. School discipline should remain a private affair.

The door opened, and Jay and Katie Irving came out, with their son Leland. From all accounts, Leland was a serious student. His presence in Ralph's office surprised Clarinda.

"Are you sure I can't change your mind?" Ralph asked.

"I'm sure," Leland said. "Thank you, Mr. Quincy, for helping me get my diploma."

Clarinda caught Ralph's hesitation, although she doubted if the others did.

"You earned it. You completed all your credit hours, although colleges like to see that final semester of English and calculus."

"I'll worry about that after the war. I can't think of any

reason why I should stay here, sitting in class, when over in Europe our boys are fighting and dying every day."

With a final handshake, Leland left.

"Mrs. Finch, Betty, good to see you. How can I help you?" Ralph held open the door and then held the backs of the chairs, first for Clarinda, then for Betty.

Betty patted her mother's hand, and Clarinda laid the briefcase in her lap. "I have the transcripts and other information for the girls who are transferring to Maple Notch High School next semester." Her voice quavered. Pushing past her uneasiness, Clarinda pulled the folders out of the briefcase. "Six in all. Betty and Norma, as well as four other local girls. You're lucky to get them." Her voice caught in her throat but she handed the folders across the desk.

"I know we are." Ralph's voice held only quiet restraint. "So let me see."

"I have arranged them in order of their anticipated dates of graduation, starting with the oldest."

"That would be me." Betty gestured to herself. "And my friend Wilma Thomas." She stood. "You may want to discuss my transcript in private. I'll step out for a few minutes." She flashed one of those smiles that would have every boy swooning over her within days of entering the school, Clarinda was sure. Children had to grow up, but Betty had far, far too soon. Norma was close behind.

"I may have some questions for you," Ralph said.

"I won't stay away long." Betty disappeared through the door.

Ralph flipped through the folders. Two seniors, a junior, a freshman, Clarinda's daughter Norma, one from junior high. "Everything appears to be in order. I will make sure we have openings in the classes they requested, but I don't anticipate a problem."

"Good." Clarinda relaxed. The transition had gone more smoothly than she had expected. "You probably noticed that one student's math grades are questionable, that of my daughter Norma. You may wish to test her skill level before placing her in with the other freshmen."

"If you believe it's necessary." Ralph made a note in Norma's file.

"I believe so." Clarinda nodded. "We could work on it during Christmas vacation."

Norma would do anything she needed to improve her grades. Without it, her hopes of earning babysitting money disappeared. She had even devised a plan to take care of their boarders' children so that no one girl would be up late more than twice a week. Clarinda wanted to reward her diligence.

"Can she come after school today, then, to meet with the math teacher? If she needs help over Christmas break…" Clarinda said.

"I'd appreciate it."

"I should have brought these things to you sooner, but it took longer than I expected to put things together for everyone, and my priority was the girls transferring to another boarding school."

"Of course." Ralph closed the folders. "Can I help you with anything else?"

"Not at this time." Now to escape before the tears began. "Call me if you have any questions, if you need help, in any way at all." Clarinda hurried from the room.

Shortly thereafter Clarinda had faced an even harder goodbye. Aunt Flo had suffered a sudden heart attack and died. The loss had drained Clarinda of all her reserves, and now Arthur was leaving for basic training tomorrow.

For Clarinda, 1942 couldn't end soon enough. America had gone to war, the two pillars in her life—husband

and aunt—had died, and her two sons had joined the battle. Not only that, but the seminary had closed its doors after seventy-five years. If one year had brought so many changes, what lay ahead in 1943? For the first time in her life, she wondered if she could go on.

New Year's Day fell on a Thursday, and people looked forward to an extended weekend to celebrate the occasion. The funds raised from the annual gala were marked for the war effort, and from what Ralph had seen, the planning committee had prepared a full evening.

"Are you sure this circus is a good idea, with the children running it?" Clarinda fretted. "At least it's indoors, where people won't get cold."

"Of course. I think it's wildly creative. I can't wait to see what Anita and the other children have put together."

"I'm as nervous as if I'm the one going onstage. I made myself take part in my senior play. Never again, I promised."

Ralph flicked his eyes over her. "For someone who speaks and debates as well as you do, that seems unlikely."

"Skills borne out of sheer terror." She smiled. "Words are weapons. Pretending to be in a circus is a different art, one at which I'm not skilled."

Anita had come up with the idea as a way to raise additional money for the war effort. According to Clarinda, Anita had also asked for war bonds for Christmas. That didn't surprise him. Schoolchildren were among America's most patriotic citizens.

Family, friends and the just plain curious filled the school gymnasium, leaving the students with a space the size of the basketball court for their performance. The locker rooms served as changing and staging areas. Ralph looked at the packed stands, wondering where he would sit, when he spotted Betty holding several empty places in the front row. When she looked up, she waved them over.

"Hi, Mr. Quincy." Betty wore a hat made out of newspaper, painted bright yellow, with a string tied under her chin. "How do you like my circus hat?"

Ralph laughed. He helped Clarinda sit, then joined her on the bench.

"Oh, wait, here comes Anita."

Anita came out in a black suit jacket over red pants.

Clarinda pointed to the tall black top hat on Anita's head. "She made the hat out of cardboard. I hope it stays on her head for the night."

Anita tapped on the mike and spoke in a high-pitched voice. "Ladies and gentlemen, children of all ages, welcome to the Maple Notch Elementary School Circus. We have colorful clowns, dazzling dogs, hopping horses, fear-inducing feats of acrobatics and even a crazy cat or two."

"The alliteration was her idea." Clarinda whispered.

Ralph suspected Clarinda would offer a blow-by-blow description of each act. Instead, Clarinda settled back to enjoy the rest of the show.

The number of live animals in the parade surprised Ralph. Had the children promised to clean up later, or did that delightful deployment fall to the parents? The clowns dressed in hobo outfits and oversize clothes, their face paint emphasizing red noses and white faces. A couple had wigs with outrageous colors, and the littlest had an actual clown costume.

A clown act opened the show, hobos fighting over a cart painted a garish yellow. The sight of children crawling in, over and under the pony-drawn cart brought a few laughs.

"Do you know any of the children? I know most of Anita's classmates, but I haven't remained as connected with the younger classes." Clarinda studied the program.

"Although the names are familiar, and several of them are distant cousins."

Ralph studied the list. Grinning, he pointed to the tallest lad, trying to pull the pony cart the last few feet out of the gym. "If I had to guess, that one there is Johnny Irving, a baby brother of the young man who just decided to graduate early so that he could join the army. Firecrackers, all of them, but they turn into good men."

The thought sobered him, and some of the joy he felt in the circus oozed away. *Johnny.* That was Ralph's younger brother's name, one who'd made the same decision that Leland had—and had paid the ultimate price.

Ralph brought his attention back to the circus. Clowns scurried across the floor, sweeping, pretending to slip and fall. Animal acts came next.

Norma wandered in front of them, holding a tray full of bags. "Peanuts, get your circus peanuts here. Fresh lemonade."

"I'll take two bags of peanuts and two drinks." Ralph gave Norma money. "Keep the change."

"Thanks, Mr. Quincy."

"I'll take one of your rain sticks." Clarinda pulled change from her purse. "I assume you want us to make noise later."

"Thanks, Mom." Norma continued up the bleachers.

"Here are the dogs. Norma said they perform some cute tricks."

Ralph had to agree. After six pups turned over, sat and played dead at the same time, their miniature handler led three through a series of hoops and over obstacles. For a final trick, she threw a rag doll in the direction of the bleachers, where it landed in Clarinda's lap. A collie/setter mix brushed against her knees and tugged the doll away from her hand. Panting, he looked at Clarinda with such a begging look that Clarinda leaned forward to pet him. "Well done, boy."

The dog wiggled all over before carrying the doll back to his handler. The audience erupted in laughter and applause. Ralph rose to his feet, and soon the others joined him.

As the noise dimmed, Clarinda struck the floor once with her rain stick—a cardboard tube filled rocks—then a second time. Soon the gym reverberated with the rhythmic striking of rain sticks and feet on the floor.

"If it snows tonight, everyone will blame you."

"Or thank me. Farmers welcome moisture, except at harvest time." Clarinda kept a smile on her face.

The circus flew by after that, with a final showing of clowns chasing after balloons and popping them. The hour approached ten o'clock. Anita, in her final moments as ringmaster, came to the center ring.

"We have raised $729 for the war effort. Thank you, Maple Notch. And now, please help me welcome the mayor of Maple Notch, and my mother, Clarinda Finch."

Clarinda walked out to the center of the floor and took the mike. "Our elementary schoolchildren deserve a big round of applause for the wonderful job they did with tonight's circus." She brought her hands together, and everyone joined in.

When the noise died down, Clarinda spoke again. "Let's leave the gymnasium in order and give our students the opportunity to prepare for the high school band and choir concert, beginning in about half an hour."

Clarinda arranged a field trip for the first town-council meeting of the New Year. Ralph surprised her by calling early that day.

"Remember when I invited you to join me for dinner a

few weeks back? We never made it to the restaurant. Are you available before tonight's meeting?"

Clarinda started to refuse, but she had promised. She couldn't imagine a better night for the "date." She had already prepared for tonight's meeting, and the children had no homework during vacation. With no good reason to decline, and several reasons to accept, she said yes.

After hanging up the phone, Clarinda headed for her closet when she came home. What should she wear? This wasn't a date—was it? Afterward, they would head for the town-council meeting, so she should dress accordingly.

Still, Clarinda tired of the tailored looks she wore morning to night, five days a week. For this—meal—with Ralph, she wanted something a little softer. She found what she was seeking: a green woolen skirt that fell in soft folds to her knees, a button-down blouse with three-quarter-length sleeves and a patterned scarf with matching colors. She tried a hat at various angles before Norma arrived at her door. "Mr. Quincy is here to see you." She looked Clarinda up and down. "You look great, Mom. Is this a *date?*"

"Who's going on a date?" Betty entered the room as Norma asked the question. "Did you take my advice, Mom?"

"Mr. Quincy is here to pick Mom up." Norma's eyes opened as wide as the ocean at high tide.

"We're on the town council together, that's all. This is no more a date than you sitting with Leland at the New Year's Eve concert was."

Betty's face colored, and too late Clarinda realized her mistake. "Oh, sweetheart, I'm sorry."

Betty shook her head. "There's nothing to be sorry for. He was leaving for the marines, and I have to finish school, and we're just too young. If we're right for each other, we'll find each other later." She reached for a tube of lipstick. "Use this, Mom. You need something with a little more flair."

Before Clarinda could object, Betty added a dash of wine-colored lipstick to her mother's lips, defining their shape and making Clarinda look alluring, not at all mayoral. "I don't know if this is such a good idea."

"Believe me, Mr. Quincy will like it," Betty said, and Norma nodded. As far as the girls were concerned, that was all that mattered.

"Now let me get downstairs. No matter what your friends may tell you, no gentleman likes to be kept waiting."

The gleam in Ralph's eye had nothing to do with their joint work on the town council, and the idea made her uncomfortable. She almost grabbed a napkin and wiped the lipstick off her lips. Instead, she turned to business. "I would invite you to see the changes we've made in preparation for our new residents and opening the nursery, but the council will be coming here tonight, and I'd show you then anyway. So…where are we headed?"

"To a restaurant in Burlington, so there won't be anyone to gossip about our meal together."

So Ralph didn't intend this as a date. The thought shouldn't bother Clarinda. Should it?

While they drove to Burlington, Ralph asked intelligent questions about the girls transferring to the public high school, showing he had studied their transcripts in detail. "How has the tutor I suggested for Norma worked out?"

"She's done an incredible job. Norma might not have cared about her grades with poor Miss Pepper, but Norma has no desire to embarrass herself in her new school. If only she had put forth the effort earlier…" Clarinda shook her head. "*Should have* and *could have* don't belong in my vocabulary."

"Sometimes I think of the *should haves* in my life." Ralph looked thoughtful.

"Such as?" Ralph exuded such confidence that Clarinda couldn't imagine him having any regrets.

He hesitated, and she wondered if the question was too personal.

"I wonder if I should have married." He glanced at her, his expression unreadable.

"It's not too late. There are plenty of women who would love to be Mrs. Ralph Quincy."

"Such as you?" His lips twitched, and Clarinda relaxed.

Twilight darkened the road, but Ralph drove with a familiarity that made Clarinda feel safe. Soon they were seated in an Italian restaurant, and Ralph recommended the chicken parmigiana. In spite of their many common projects, they didn't discuss work at all. Instead, they debated their common passion: history.

"People have started to refer to the Great War, our war, as the First World War," Clarinda said. "With the way the Japanese are rolling across the Pacific, all the world is involved in this war. Our young people have no idea what it was like back then. We had turned the tide of the war in Europe, women finally won the right to vote…anything seemed possible, for a few heady years." In her excitement, she had leaned forward. She leaned back. "Oh, to be that young and full of hope again."

"I don't know about that." Ralph met her eyes. "There is something to be said for being older and wiser. The years have only made you more beautiful."

"Oh, Ralph. And you have grown more distinguished." She blushed and turned away.

"Our blindness allowed that madman to rise to power

in Germany unopposed. We gave them enough time to get strong. And now our young men are fighting and dying." Ralph pointed at Clarinda with his knife, then relaxed. "I'm sorry. My reasons for opposing our young men running off and joining the army are personal, not professional. I can't see the situation with a clear mind, as I keep reminding myself."

Chapter 8

Ralph hadn't intended to mention personal reasons for his ongoing objections to young men joining the army before graduation. His impromptu compliment had revealed too much of his heart, and he hurried to steer attention to something else. Unfortunately, if anyone had valid personal reasons for objecting to young men enlisting before their time, it was Clarinda. Her husband dead, and both sons enlisted? She hadn't said much about Arthur's post-Christmas departure, but Ralph knew it must have been hard, especially on top of her aunt's death.

"You're talking about your brother, aren't you?" Candle-light flickered across her face. As she leaned forward, her eyes narrowed and lines formed on her cheeks.

Ralph sensed the concern of a woman, not of a mayor only focused on the war effort, and he responded to that woman. "He left school early to sign up. And yes, he died. Men die in every war, but he was so young. He didn't need to go so soon."

Clarinda nodded. "I agree. But Betty keeps reminding me that, if we don't offer ways for them to make a difference, they will find other means to get involved—like leaving school early. If Anita thought they would take a ten-year-old, she'd march into the enlistment office today."

Ralph laughed. "I'm sure she would. Children led one of the crusades of old, after all."

"You're good with children as well as our teenagers." Clarinda chewed a bite of the chicken. "I've noticed that before. Do you have any interest in being the superintendent of schools someday, so that you are over all our students?"

Smiling, Ralph shook his head. "Each so-called promotion puts more distance between me and the reason I became a teacher. Tell me, which do you prefer, the classroom or the office?"

Clarinda pursed her mouth as she considered his question. "I'm not sure. Can I make a confession?" She flicked her eyes around the room as if wondering who might be listening.

"What's that?" Ralph couldn't imagine Clarinda saying anything embarrassing.

"When I used to teach from time to time…when I first took over the position of mayor…I liked it. I enjoy working, but I feel guilty when Anita doesn't get to bed on time or Norma does poorly or Betty wants…the world."

"All Betty wants is to grow up. We may feel it's too soon, but it's not in our control. Not entirely."

Their conversation drifted onto other topics, and all too soon, they finished their meal. By the time they reached the seminary, the rest of the town council was waiting for them. More time had passed than Ralph had expected. Instead of being early, Clarinda was late to a town-council meeting for the first time. If he had wanted to draw attention to their meal together, he couldn't have devised a better plan.

"I'll be back in a few minutes. Please excuse me, gentlemen." Clarinda disappeared in the direction of the back bedrooms.

None of the men said anything while they waited, although Rich glanced at Ralph. "Later." Ralph mouthed the word. Besides, what was there to tell? Nothing. Two friends and coworkers shared a meal.

After Clarinda returned, she led them to the second floor. "When we received the boardinghouse applications, it became apparent that the greatest need was larger rooms for women with small children."

The aroma of fresh-sawed wood and varnish filled Ralph's nostrils, and fresh wallpaper brightened the rooms.

"We added an extra full bath on this hall, as well as upstairs, and installed a larger hot-water heater. We transformed a dozen rooms into seven on this floor and added three more upstairs, for a total of ten. Ten women and fifteen children will occupy the house and take their meals with us."

The council peppered her with questions, but Clarinda had ready answers. The rooms themselves were inviting. Half of the rooms held baby cribs. That brought up another concern: What about the children?

Clarinda took them to the first floor, where they had converted one of the classrooms into a child's playroom, a haven for any curious youngster. A working calendar hung on the wall. Residents, the pastor's wife and several teenagers would divide the duties. It was well organized, as Ralph expected of anything Clarinda created.

"We hope to provide a homelike environment for both the women and their children. Our 'Rosie Riveters' are performing such an important duty for our country, many with husbands serving overseas. We hope to make their new home as welcoming as possible."

"Speaking of warm welcomes, I have gathered baskets with coupons from several of our local merchants to give to your new residents," Rich said. "I'll bring them over tomorrow. They're a token of the goodwill of the community."

"Why, thank you, Mr. Adams."

Congratulations swirled around Clarinda. Ralph wondered if he was the only one to sense potential problems with the new arrangement.

The new residents moved in over the weekend. In the end, Clarinda accepted all the applications she had reviewed with Ralph. She felt obligated to accept Audrey Smith, the former mayor's daughter-in-law who had a small child and worked at the factory. Hattie Charles's lack of even basic writing skills bothered Clarinda but didn't affect her value as a resident. Carol, Daisy and Edna all came well recommended.

Each married woman came with one or more children. Clarinda had also accepted a number of single women as residents. She had prayed over each application, seeking God's will—more than she did most years in considering new students for the seminary. Perhaps because after all this time she could identify a seminary girl. Rosie the Riveter was a new commodity, drawn from a broad range of age, experience and education.

All of these young women claimed church membership. Clarinda prayed their common faith would see them through any difficulties.

Audrey Smith checked in last, with an eighteen-month-old still in diapers. Bill Smith, the former mayor, accompanied his daughter-in-law. "I appreciate your taking in

Audrey and Trey. They're welcome in our house, as long as they wish, of course, but this is definitely more convenient."

Behind Bill, Audrey struggled with a playpen. Betty dashed forward and helped ease the final corner out of the truck bed. The moving boxes reached shoulder high, and Clarinda wondered where she would fit everything.

"Let's get your things inside." Clarinda rubbed her hands together and picked up the top box. Since it was marked *Fragile,* she assumed it had figurines or some such. Hopefully the small children in the house wouldn't decide to play with them. Clarinda had swept through the house with her girls, storing the most breakable and irreplaceable items in the attic.

"I can manage that box." Audrey took the box from Clarinda's hands.

"That's all right...." Clarinda's voice trailed after Audrey's back. "You have the second room to the right at the top of the stairs." She grabbed another box, this one filled with clothes, and headed for the stairs. As she felt her way up the steps, some of the excitement that she felt at the beginning of the fall semester put a bounce in her gait. New adventures lay ahead.

Clarinda almost tripped over the box Audrey had left at the top of the stairs. As for Audrey herself, she stood at the door to her room, studying it as if deciding whether or not to accept the accommodations.

"Is there a problem?" Clarinda asked.

Audrey glanced at Clarinda over her shoulder. "I, uh, was expecting something a little bigger. I had my eye on the room at the end of the hall."

"We assigned rooms based on need. The lady in the corner room has three children with her and was in desperate need of the additional space." Clarinda kept a smile in her voice. So far, no one else had complained about the room assignments.

Audrey continued, unaware of the impression she was making. "And I was hoping for a room with a window on the backyard. So much more interesting than the street."

Clarinda preferred the view of the town square herself but hadn't factored the view in room assignments. "The rest of the residents are already settled. Let us help you get your things moved and set up, and it will feel like home in no time at all."

"I suppose I can ask Mrs.—" Audrey crossed the hall and read the name card Clarinda had placed outside the door "—Mrs. Charles if she is willing to change places with me later."

Clarinda would put a stop to that plan but for now helped Audrey move in. Dresses hung on every hanger, and Audrey folded a few sweaters alongside baby clothes in a bureau drawer. The boy had cute outfits. A pair of dungarees embroidered with *William Smith III* caught Clarinda's eye. So "Trey" was a nickname.

About midway through the boxes, Audrey stopped unpacking and studied the remaining space. She walked to the washstand in the corner, fingering the towels hung at the side. "I thought each room would have a private bath."

"Oh, no, although we have increased the number of baths to make it easier for everyone. It's just two doors down the hall, on the left."

"If I must." Audrey brushed past Clarinda on the way to the commode. Clarinda let out her breath, striving to release her resentment over Audrey's unreasonable demands.

"She really does appreciate having a room here." Bill wiped his forehead with a handkerchief. "You've done an amazing job transforming the old rooms."

Clarinda smiled. Bill had a good heart. "Does Audrey

or Trey have any special dietary needs we need to be aware of?"

Bill shook his head. "Not that I know of."

Organizing Audrey's room took the remainder of Saturday afternoon, finding a place for Trey's last toy car as the dinner bell rung.

"Lovely!" Clarinda said. "A hot, refreshing dinner sounds like just the thing to restore my spirits. I believe our cook has Boston baked beans for us this evening."

"Because it's Saturday night?" Audrey's face crumpled. "That will be okay, I guess."

Lord, give me patience.

"So Audrey wanted Hattie's room?" Ralph shook his head as he reviewed his lesson plans for Hattie and the other workers—not all of them boarders, he was pleased to note—who had decided to attend the GED preparation class.

Clarinda nodded. "Hattie has a heart of gold. She would have given the mayor's daughter-in-law her room if I hadn't stepped in and said no. Hattie needs the space more than Audrey does, and that's that." She paused. "Hattie is also really excited about beginning the GED class."

Ralph scratched his head. "She's settled down since high school. Back then, all she could think about was Mark, the man she ended up marrying."

"People used to ask Grandma Clara about marriage. Since she so strongly believed in things like education and suffrage for women, sometimes people thought she might feel like marriage held a woman back. But she said no. Marriage to the right man made the woman stronger."

"And as they say, behind every great man stands a woman. How about Eleanor Roosevelt, for example." How might his life be different now if he had married? Instead of his high school sweetheart, Clarinda filled his mind.

Clarinda nodded absentmindedly, unaware of the thoughts parading through his head. The page in front of her was filled with black lines and empty spaces, names written in every available space, with half of them crossed out.

"What is that? Can I help?" Ralph asked.

Clarinda shook her head. "I don't think so. I am trying to work out a schedule for chores. All the residents are responsible for keeping the common areas clean, their own laundry, two meals a day. And of course the nursery."

She turned over the pad. "So far, running Maple Notch is easier than running a boardinghouse. We didn't have a problem with the students. It's included in the residency contracts, so I didn't expect so much difficulty. I'd send them home if I could, but what would happen to the children?"

"It always comes down to the children, doesn't it? Whenever I wonder if I am doing anything important, I remind myself of Jesus's words about letting the little children come to Him. What a child learns, how he thinks about himself, when he's young, shapes his whole life. I'm sure the children you are taking in along with their mothers will remember these days with fondness. You're offering an important service."

As he said the words, the door opened to a girl of about three. Her eyes widened when she saw the two adults sitting there. "Can I hide in here?" she asked in a whisper loud enough to give her away to the person searching for her.

Clarinda stood and crossed the room. "I'm afraid not. This is a private room. But I know a good place to hide." Holding the girl's hand, she walked out the door, the botched schedule still on her desk. Instead of making things easier for Clarinda, the closure of the seminary had increased her burden. Not that she would ever complain or ask for help.

A couple of the unmarried residents wanted to volunteer as plane spotters in addition to their factory jobs. The overlapping schedules meant Ralph and Clarinda had to coordinate their calendars. Perhaps he could help. If she objected, he would deal with it later.

He studied the paper where Clarinda had attempted her division of duties on a calendar grid. The page where she had indicated what hours each resident worked as well as which children needed care remained neat and unremarkable.

The next few pages, however, overflowed with confusion. Weekends presented some difficulty. Babysitting was needed even on Sunday mornings, when the women who worked the night shift on Saturday needed to rest. But since high school students worked primarily on the weekends, that wasn't the biggest problem.

Clarinda's careful penmanship mocked her questions. *Adult supervision? Me?* appeared more than once. *Audrey— nothing after 9:00 p.m.* and similar notes about other residents took up more space than the hours they could work.

Ralph took fresh paper and marked six pages, Monday through Saturday, in hour-long segments. From there, he entered the names and schedules of each resident. He hunted through the desk for a red pencil to mark their preferred volunteer hours.

The problem was, some hours and chores had no one available to cover. Residents would have to give up some of their free time. He doubted adults would appreciate the interference any better than high school students did, but they must work together for the boardinghouse to function. He divided the number of chore hours among the adult residents. Each should shoulder an equal number of responsibilities. To achieve that, he went back through the schedule, marking out some of the notes made by his red pencil.

The door swished open, and Ralph twisted around, expecting to see Clarinda. Instead, Audrey approached and glanced over his shoulder at the schedule. "I told Mrs. Finch I can't work after nine at night, so why did she write me down?"

Ralph sucked in his breath. "Actually, I proposed this schedule. You must carry your fair share of the load. Feel free to look it over."

Chapter 9

Clarinda stood at the end of the hall, listening to Ralph explain the schedule to Audrey. She appreciated his support, but she should handle her own problems. Shouldn't she? She sped down the hall and joined the conversation.

"Mrs. Smith, I am so glad you are here." Clarinda glanced at the schedule in Ralph's hand. She would examine it later. "I have decided to hold a resident-council meeting this evening, before the overnight shift leaves for work. Everyone will have a chance to voice their concerns at that time. For now, I ask that you keep your complaints to yourself." She glanced at the schedule again. "It looks like you have free time this afternoon, and the laundry is clear. You may wish to take advantage of it."

Audrey hesitated a moment before she turned on her heels. She twisted around long enough to say, "I'll be there tonight, ready with my opinions."

"I look forward to it." Clarinda waited until Audrey

reached the stairs before sitting down. Ralph's schedule wouldn't satisfy everyone, but she already knew that wasn't possible. After studying the page a few minutes, she said, "I should have been able to do this. Thanks for your help." She was depending on Ralph more and more, and it made her uncomfortable.

"I'm glad to do it. Sometimes I stare at class schedules until I'm blind, and then my secretary finds the answer right away. A second set of eyes is always welcome."

When he put it like that, how could she refuse? "Dealing with the residents is so different from the seminary. There, if someone misbehaved, I had a certain amount of authority. I suppose I could threaten to make a troublemaker leave, but that's like admitting we made a mistake." She wiped her hand across her forehead. "I'm sure Grandma Clara had problems to iron out at first, as well."

"Forming a resident council sounds like a good idea. Democracy works. They can come to common solutions that they might not on their own."

"I hope so." Clarinda gathered her useless papers and ripped them in half with a satisfying tear. Ralph chuckled, and she looked at him, embarrassed. "Sometimes it helps."

He nodded. "We'll have two training sessions for the plane spotters on Saturday, one in the morning, one in the afternoon. I've left notes for the women who were interested." He nodded in the direction of the mail cubbyholes. "We'll start soon after that. If you don't mind, I'll make a note of the times your residents are scheduled to work around here so that I can plan accordingly." He wrote a few names and times in his notebook before standing. "Good luck with the resident council. I'll see you on Thursday, if not before."

Clarinda walked with him to the door. "Good night, Ralph. And thanks again." She watched him as he walked away, his head tilted a little to the side, probably whistling as he so often did. Would she see him tomorrow? She didn't know—and she realized she had come to look forward to their almost daily visits.

Later that night, the residents gathered in the parlor. Betty had prepared copies of the agenda, the resident agreement, which they had signed before moving in, and the schedule Ralph had worked out with only a few changes.

By the time Audrey arrived, the only remaining seat was the chair next to Clarinda, but she didn't seem to mind. All the residents not at work, seven of them in all, had come to the meeting. "Welcome to the first resident-council meeting of the Bailey Boardinghouse. Let's start with a word of prayer, shall we?" Clarinda's heart went with her words as she asked God to direct their thoughts and decisions on that evening.

Betty passed out the pages she had prepared as Clarinda introduced the reason for the meeting. "It is to be expected that we need to make a few adjustments as we settle into this new environment. For some of you, this is your first experience in community living. It is definitely different, as difficult as sharing a bathroom with seven sisters, except that you aren't even related. I appreciate all the patience that you have already shown."

Most of the women smiled, and a few clapped.

"Let's look at the resident agreement, which you all signed before moving in. I want to highlight a few things. Let's turn to the resident's-responsibilities page. I draw your attention to items three through five, which I have underlined." The paragraphs mentioned the need for residents to maintain their rooms and the common areas, including the ubiquitous "and other duties as assigned," which was the escape clause of so many legal agreements. No single list could ever cover all problems that might exist.

Audrey flipped through the pages. When Clarinda asked if anyone had questions, she raised her hand immediately. "I see that under 'resident rights,' we have the right to dispute any assigned duties. Who do we take our complaints to?"

Clarinda counted to ten quickly. "That is the purpose of this meeting. You can raise questions here. The group may prefer to elect representatives to hear your complaints and then bring them to me." She smiled her most polite, crowd-pleasing, conciliatory smile, which she had perfected over the past year. "But before we discuss complaints, let's go through the schedule."

Using her most neutral voice, Clarinda pointed to the clause that stated single residents could be asked to work up to five hours, while mothers would do an additional hour for each child in the family. "It is acceptable to swap your hours with another resident, but everyone is expected to work their hours at some point during the week."

"You should have seen the look in Audrey's eyes when we went over the rights and responsibilities of residents. She acted like she hadn't read them before she signed the agreement."

At least Clarinda laughed as she reported on the resident-council meeting. "You say they elected her as one of the representatives?" Ralph took a satisfying bite of egg salad sandwich, the perfect blend of egg, mayonnaise, mustard and relish. After he finished the sandwich, he folded the bag and put it in his briefcase.

"Audrey represents the day shift. There is one from every shift, and they'll meet with me once a week."

"I suppose that's best. She'll see how hard it is to accommodate everyone."

"I hope so." Clarinda sobered a bit. "She worked her scheduled shift, along with Norma, in the nursery last night."

A worried look passed over her face.

"How are your girls adjusting to the change?"

Clarinda chewed her apple to the core and threw it in the trash can before she answered. "Betty loves it. She's so anxious to start the plane-spotter program that she's doing things even before I ask."

"She's doing well at high school from what I've seen. Of course, she went to elementary school with most of the students, and she's participated in youth activities at church, so she's always been involved." He wondered whether he should say anything else. "I'm proud to have her at the high school."

Clarinda's pleased smile let him know that his praise of her daughter was appreciated. Then her grin faded. "How is Norma doing? She hasn't said much."

"She's quieter," Ralph said. "Her algebra teacher reports that she is doing well, so she has taken that challenge to heart."

"Good. She's organized babysitting duties for the high school girls. She's a good administrator, it appears, which I would never have guessed if she hadn't been given the opportunity."

Betty was exceeding expectations, Norma was doing well in other areas, so the problem must be…Anita.

"Of course, Anita's not in high school yet, so I don't know her as well." Ralph unwrapped a cracker and nibbled on it.

Clarinda sighed. "She's the only elementary schoolchild in the house, unless you count the kindergarten students.

But we've had to put a few areas off-limits to any of the children. She resents it. She'd rather be out on the farm." She sighed. "And we didn't get out there over Christmas break, between Aunt Flo's death and converting the rooms and everything." Her voice trailed off, and she looked at Ralph. "Am I a bad mother for putting the town and the school ahead of my own children?"

Ralph shifted in his seat. "What do I know about being a mother? Whatever you think, you are a strong woman doing an incredible job in a difficult situation. Would it help if I did the weekly schedule, since I already have to do it for the plane-spotter volunteers? Would that give you more time to spend with Anita?"

"You're already doing so much," Clarinda protested.

"I consider it a privilege. I'm not trying to raise a family without a father in the middle of a war."

At least she had agreed, albeit reluctantly, before he left Clarinda's office a few minutes later. Ralph stopped at Hazel's desk and rapped his knuckles. "Thanks for calling me," he said in a low voice. "I'll be by as often as I can."

"Thanks," she whispered back.

Clarinda came out of the office. "I thought you left?"

Ralph pulled on his coat. "Just talking with Hazel about the meeting on Thursday." He winked at her. "Until tomorrow, then."

Ralph didn't see Clarinda again until the council meeting, but he swung by her office again on Friday. "I have found someone to help with the babysitting. Mrs. Anderson retired last spring, but she's been looking for something to do. I told her about the difficulties you've had with babysitting at night, and she would love to help. She'll be calling you this afternoon to discuss it with you."

Clarinda opened her mouth as if ready to protest. "Evenings are the most difficult. I will talk with her. Once again you helped."

He laughed at her. "Don't worry. I'll call on you when we get the plane-spotting program up and going." He grinned. "Are you still planning on attending the orientation program on Saturday?"

"Of course. Everyone on the town council is. I've even spent time learning the cards. I plan on being your star pupil, you know." Her voice was serious, but he saw the laughter in her eyes.

"Good. Your leadership in the endeavor has given it a lot of validity in the eyes of the community."

Clarinda called Ralph on Saturday morning. "I'm so sorry. I can't come this morning. I will come this afternoon, if I can."

Remembering their lunchtime discussion, Clarinda's announcement worried Ralph. "Has something happened that I should know about?"

"No, I just had something come up."

Something personal, which she didn't want to discuss with him. The fact she didn't tell him hurt a little, but maybe she would share the information in time.

Even without Clarinda, two dozen volunteers came to the morning training session, including Betty. "Is everything all right at home?" he asked.

She glanced away before answering. "Everything will be all right. Mom gave me her cards—I've been studying them."

Betty didn't want to tell him, either, but things couldn't be too serious if she was attending the training. He turned his mind away from Clarinda's troubles and focused on the students in his class.

By the time the first training session ended, the class could identify most of the planes in the sample air-raid shot, and twenty of twenty-four hands shot into the air for each picture he asked them to identify. Those twenty, including Betty, qualified for immediate service. The other four would work with partners until they felt more comfortable.

Maple Notch's plane-spotter program had officially begun.

I should have seen this coming.

Anita was missing. Clarinda paced about the kitchen, where the residents had gathered with her, uncertain what to do next. She had searched every nook and cranny, even the ones Anita thought Clarinda didn't know about, but didn't find Anita.

At that point, Clarinda had called Ralph to cancel her participation in training before enlisting every available resident in a second search of the house. After an hour, they gave up.

"Don't worry, Mrs. Finch. I'm sure she's just gone to visit a friend or something like that." Hattie's attempted reassurance didn't assuage Clarinda's fears.

Norma had asked Clarinda to call Anita's friends, as well as her aunts and uncles. "We've already checked," Clarinda said. "And she took half a loaf of bread." She crumpled onto a chair and buried her face in her hands. "What do I do now?"

Norma took the last chair at the kitchen table. "We pray. Isn't that what you always tell us to do, when we have a problem?"

"Of course." Clarinda straightened in her chair. "Although I don't know if I can pray. This is one of those times that the Holy Spirit will have to take my heart and give it to God." A sob hiccuped in her throat. "Oh, Anita. Why did you have to choose now to do something foolish?"

Hattie cleared her throat. "It doesn't seem like she's being foolish to me. She has her coat and boots—I checked—and she took food. I don't think she plans on being gone very long. Maybe she just wants to have an adventure." With a hand on Clarinda's shoulder, Hattie prayed, and several other residents added their prayers. Norma ended the circle, also putting her hand on her mother's shoulder.

The prayer time gave Clarinda strength to get moving. "Norma, I need you to stay here, in case Anita comes back. I'm going to the farm, to see if she went home. She's been talking about it a lot." Clarinda grabbed a change of clothes and a thermos of hot soup to take with her and then left.

As she drove, Clarinda kept pressing down and easing up on the gas pedal, wanting to eat up the road between town and the farm, determined not to miss any signs that Anita had passed this way. The day was cold but bright. As long as Anita had dressed warmly and kept moving, the weather shouldn't be a factor. *Thank You, God, for small favors.*

None of Clarinda's children had ever run away, unless she counted the time Howie and Arthur disappeared to the fishing hole for the day without telling her. She had known where they were all along, although they had considered it a grand adventure. Maybe that was all Anita had planned, to be gone for a few hours and come back tonight.

But the boys had chosen a warm summer day for their adventure, and Clarinda had felt safe, knowing where to find them. Howard called it "spreading their wings."

Today's escapade told Clarinda one thing. One way or another, she had to make more time with the girls. Didn't the Bible talk about a leader being a good ruler of his own household first of all?

When Clarinda arrived at the house, nothing indicated anyone had been there for weeks. Wallace and Mary Anne took care of the animals at the farm. Aside from keeping the house warm enough to prevent pipes from bursting, Clarinda hadn't been to the farm since the fall semester had begun.

"Anita? Are you here?" Clarinda put as much hope and strength as she could into her cry.

Only a breeze rustled the empty branches in reply. Clarinda walked into the house, breathing in the familiar scents, touching the furniture like touchstones to her past.

The stove remained unlit, and Clarinda went to the living room next. Memories came alive of family nights around the radio. Howard read the same books over and over again, at the children's request. He held Anita in his lap—his youngest, the miracle child who'd survived when her twin hadn't—and rocked her to sleep many a time. Clarinda lifted the blanket from the chair, as if expecting to uncover the pair of them.

Upstairs, she went into the boys' room, then the bedroom that Betty and Norma had shared. Betty's diary fluttered open, tempting Clarinda to read her fifteen-year-old secrets. Another time, perhaps.

Standing at the stairwell, winding downstairs and up to the attic, Clarinda called again. "Anita? Are you here?" The answering echo mocked her.

Clarinda steeled herself to enter the only remaining room on the second floor, the nursery that had been converted into Anita's bedroom as she grew. Clarinda sat in the rocking chair where Howard had spent so many sleepless nights when Anita was a baby and death seemed just a few short breaths away. She had survived the threat of early birth and her tiny size. Maybe because of her difficult beginning, they had tended to baby their youngest. *Lord, take care of Anita.* The prayer hadn't changed much over the years.

In a final, desperate hope, Clarinda climbed the attic stairs. The room belonged by rights to the eldest child remaining at home. Most recently Anita had held a pajama party in the attic for her last birthday party. Clarinda had spent the night downstairs, listening to the girlish laughter and feeling a little eased from Howard's death.

Oh, Howard, I have failed you. I have failed our girl. Lord, help me find Anita.

Chapter 10

Ralph signed the final certificate, made out to *Elizabeth Finch,* and smiled at Betty. "Congratulations. You'll make a fine plane spotter."

She didn't look as pleased as Ralph had expected, since she had overflowed with excitement when she had heard about the opportunity. Something was definitely wrong at the Finch household. "Something's going on, I can tell. Do you want to talk about it? After—" He nodded at the others who crowded around the table, examining the books he had provided for additional information, as well as the ties and scarves he promised to provide for anyone who completed the training and twenty hours of volunteer service. "After the others have left?"

"If Mom hasn't come by then." Betty spread out the deck of cards in a game of solitaire, handling them as deftly as she would an ordinary set. The girl who would work as her partner, Imogene, sat down next to her. Betty involved her in finding the matches for the game. She was patient, a good teacher, a lot like her mother. That might explain their frequent clashes.

A few minutes later, Imogene left with her mother, and the others trailed after them. Only Betty remained.

"Let's go outside." Ralph headed for the parking lot.

Betty followed him. "Mom probably doesn't want me telling you." She looked toward the Bailey Boardinghouse. "But I was praying Mom would be here when the class finished. I'm getting worried."

"Let's walk toward your home while we talk." The temperature hovered right above freezing, teasing them that the ice might melt. "If something is that wrong, I'm sure anyone on the town council is willing to help."

"Anita ran away this morning." Betty blurted the news out. "They looked all up and down the house this morning. When I left, Mom was heading to the farm. If Anita's not there, I don't know where she is."

"Oh, Betty." Ralph closed his eyes, imagining the worry that must be flooding Clarinda. "But running away from home can almost be seen as a rite of passage for children. From what I know of Anita, she has a good head on her shoulders. She knows how to take care of herself."

Betty gave him the scathing look that he deserved for that remark. "But she's the baby. When Howie used to act all grown-up, we teased him about it. I guess I did, too, since I'm the oldest girl. The point is, we both know how to do all kinds of things that Anita has never tried. She's got a great imagination, but I'm not so sure she can take care of herself."

"As long as she can ask herself 'what would Anne Shirley do,' I expect she'll be all right. I only have a couple of hours before the afternoon class starts, but I can ask around—"

Betty shook her head vehemently. "That's the last thing Mom wants."

Enough of this. "Anita needs to be home before dark. The overnight temperatures pose the biggest threat. If we haven't seen her before I have to return to class, I will tell the constable what has happened."

"That's okay. I guess." Betty frowned. "I'd better get home, or else people will start wondering what has happened to me." Her laughter sounded brittle. A faraway enemy diminished in perspective when her immediate family was in imminent danger. Ralph patted her on the shoulder, before they went their separate ways. So Anita hadn't been found at the Bailey Boardinghouse or the farm. Where else might an imaginative ten-year-old go to run away?

A couple of places came to mind. Ralph headed west, slowing down when he reached the bridge across the Bumblebee River. The bridge had ties to Clarinda's family that went back more than a hundred years, the kind of place that could inspire a child's imagination. Anita could find a dozen hiding places in the shadowed interior, but he saw no sign of her presence. Only the screech of an owl indicated any sign of life.

After the slow traverse, Ralph continued his drive in the direction of the old road, hardly more than a footpath, which led to the Tuttle cemetery. He decided against going farther. Surely Clarinda's brother, Wallace, must have searched this side of the river by now.

Something flashed as Ralph approached the bridge heading east, something he hadn't noticed before. He pulled his car to the side of the road and got out, swiveling his head to find what caused the flash. A single tin can hung from a branch of a denuded maple by the river. That might have caused the glint and not Anita after all.

Time had sped by too fast. Already he needed to return for the afternoon training session. He offered a prayer equal parts plea and frustration when he heard a rock skipping across the ground. He froze, hoping whatever had caused the sound showed itself. A dark head popped up over the edge of the riverbank before it disappeared again.

"Anita." Memories surged through Ralph of the perfect hiding place. He made his way down the snowy bank until he reached the edge of the water. Underneath the tall embankment he saw the light of a fire through an opening in the dirt.

"It's Mr. Quincy, Anita. I know you're in there." He bent over and entered.

Anita was bundled warmly, enjoying a peanut butter sandwich. An apple core burned in the fire pit. A notebook lay to one side, its pages filled with her schoolgirl script. "It took someone long enough to find me. I wasn't expecting *you*." She unfolded her legs and put away the rest of her lunch.

Members of the extended Tuttle family had taken refuge in the cave since the Revolutionary War. Ralph wondered why Clarinda hadn't checked it out, but she probably wasn't thinking straight when she was so worried.

"I put up the tin can," Anita said. "That's always been the signal. I wondered if anyone even knew I was gone."

"You told Mr. Quincy about Anita?" Clarinda demanded.

Betty stared straight at her mother. "Yes, I did. We needed help." She reached for the phone. "I'm going to call the constable, before it gets dark."

Call the constable? Clarinda might as well call Rusty Henshaw at the newspaper as get the police involved. How could the people of Maple Notch trust her with their town if they couldn't trust her with her own daughter?

What kind of mother was she, if she was more worried about what people thought than about Anita's well-being? "Before we do, let's drive out to the farm one more time. You might see something I missed."

"As long as you promise to go straight to the constable if we don't find her. We need to check with Mr. Quincy, too." Betty scooted over to make space for Norma in the backseat. When they reached the bridge, Norma made a soft cry.

Clarinda braked.

"The sign is up. Stop on the other side of the bridge."

What sign? Clarinda wondered but didn't question. She pulled the car to the side of the road and Norma sprang from the car.

"What is it?" Clarinda hurried after Norma, Betty on her heels.

Norma pointed to the single tin can dangling from the maple tree. "We always hang a tin can from the tree if we go to the cave. Anita must be there." She sprinted ahead of her mother.

By the time Clarinda reached the riverbank, Norma had climbed back to the top. "She was there earlier. There are ashes from the fire. But she's gone."

"Someone parked on this side of the road," Betty said. "I can see the tire tracks in the snow. Maybe it's Mr. Quincy, and they're back at the house."

Clarinda debated. Should she go on to the farmhouse? Go to Wallace's home to use the phone? What if Ralph hadn't found her? What if it was some stranger, someone who meant harm…? Heart in her throat, Clarinda sent up a quick prayer for wisdom. A glance at her watch confirmed that the second training session had started. Even if Ralph had found Anita, he wouldn't be waiting with her at home.

"Go home," Betty said. "I'll go to the school where Mr. Quincy is teaching. Maybe he has Anita with him. I'll call you as soon as I find out so we can…you know. Talk with the constable."

Clarinda saw no point in waiting, so the three of them climbed into the car. When they reached home, Betty jumped out first. "I'll call when I reach the school. Ten minutes, maybe less."

Norma reached the front door first and squealed as soon as she got inside. When Clarinda saw Anita's favorite red coat hanging on the coat tree, Clarinda wanted to squeal herself.

"We're in here." Hattie's voice floated to them from the kitchen.

Clarinda pulled her coat off her arms as she raced down the hall. Anita sat next to the stove, a big mug of hot cocoa and a small plate with chocolate chip cookies in front of her. A knapsack lay by her feet, the peanut butter jar peeking out of the top.

Clarinda didn't know whether to scream or cry, and instead she laughed. "You have led us on a merry chase today."

Anita rolled her eyes. "I expected you to find me."

"I know. I saw the can," Norma said. "But I guess Mom didn't know about our sign. Now we'll have to change it." She smiled as if keeping secrets was a good thing.

"But instead of you, Mr. Quincy found me." Anita sounded cross, as if Clarinda had done something wrong.

Worry-fueled rage burned up inside of Clarinda, and she feared she would explode. Instead she counted to ten. "Do you have any more of that hot cocoa for the two of us, Hattie?"

"Coming right up." Hattie rattled with the cups and made enough noise to make conversation difficult. Anita nibbled her cookies a bite at a time while they waited.

Hattie set hot cocoa and cookies in front of them after a few minutes. "I'll be in my room, if you need me."

Clarinda waited until Hattie had left. "We'll talk about appropriate discipline later." Clarinda had decided that much. "You can't run away and have all of us worried about you like that, not without consequences. But for right now, I just want you to know how glad I am that you are safe. I'm sorry I didn't know the secret sign. I'm sorry about a lot of things."

Anita blinked and ate another bite. "I understand. You have to do a lot of things since the war started and Dad died. I talk with the other kids at school. They say their moms are acting different while their fathers are off fighting." Her sad-looking eyes didn't match her confident words.

"But being your mother will always be the most important thing in my life. And I've forgotten that a little bit. I promise I'll make more time to be with you at night and on the weekends. Even if that means I have to stop something else."

"Even if you have to stop being the mayor?" Anita asked.

Clarinda's mouth opened but she didn't have an answer.

"That's what I thought." Anita slipped the last half cookie into her mouth and drained her cup of hot cocoa. "May I be excused?"

Two weeks had passed since Anita had run away on the same day Ralph had certified thirty-five plane spotters for Maple Notch. Clarinda had refused his company, for lunch or any other kind of meal. She had only seen him, along with all of the council members, at the Thursday-night meetings.

More focused, more driven than ever, the strain on her showed in the circles under her eyes and the weary tilt to her head. Clarinda needed a Job-like wake-up call. Her heart had broken over Anita's behavior, but her despair affected everyone around her—including the new residents.

Deena, one of the single residents who had taken a room at the house, offered to volunteer two nights a week as a plane spotter. The second time she had to cancel at the last minute, she apologized. "I thought we had our chore schedule worked out, but people keep asking me to work for them. They seem to think that, because I'm single, I can pitch in whenever there's a need. But if something doesn't change, I'll have to move somewhere else or quit the plane-spotting program."

"The resident council?" Ralph asked delicately.

"Hasn't met. They can't find a time they can all get together with Mrs. Finch. I'm ready to go back home, even if I have to drive farther. Mr. Quincy, is there anything you can do to help?"

Hazel answered when Ralph called the mayor's office. "Good morning, Mr. Quincy! Let me connect you with Mrs. Finch."

"Actually, I wanted to speak with you. I would like to make an appointment to see the mayor this afternoon, if possible."

"Give me a minute." Ralph heard pages rustling in the background, and then Hazel returned. "If you can make it here before school lets out, Mrs. Finch is free for half an hour at 2:30."

Ralph glanced at his clock and considered his own task list for the day. He'd have to cut his lunch short. "I'll be there. And, er, please don't tell her who made the appointment."

Hazel laughed. "I will try."

Ralph worked his way through lunch, holding a bologna sandwich in his left hand while he wrote down random thoughts with his right. He still hadn't hit upon an idea to lighten Clarinda's load when his secretary buzzed him. "I'm sorry to disturb you during lunch, Mr. Quincy, but Mrs. Smith says it's urgent."

Audrey Smith. Did Clarinda know she gave him as much trouble as she did her? The woman was patriotic through and through, but difficult to handle. Come to think of it, that sounded like the rebels who founded the country. He chuckled. "Go ahead and put her through."

"Mr. Quincy, I have a problem," Audrey said when she was put through.

Of course she did. "Is there something I can do to assist you?"

"Not really. But when I was driving home from my watch last night, I wasn't able to see the icy patches on the road without my headlights. My car spun out of control and went into the ditch. I barely missed hitting another car."

When Ralph heard that, he was surprised that the former mayor hadn't called to complain about road conditions.

"One of the other gals here is giving me a ride to work, but I can't make it to my shift tonight. In fact, I am wondering if I should continue."

Once the going got tough, Audrey wanted to quit? In some ways, he would say good riddance to the troublemaker, but she was the fifth person that week to tell him the schedule was more than he or she could handle.

"I'm sorry to hear that. Perhaps you could work with a partner, like Hattie. That way, if one of you misses a shift, the other one will still be there."

"Hattie?" Audrey paused long enough to let Ralph know what she thought of that idea. "I'll let you know."

After they hung up, Ralph pulled out the plane-spotter schedule and erased Deena's and Audrey's names from today's watches. He frowned. One of the senior high men had already offered to work whenever Ralph needed someone extra. That student would rather spend forty hours a week up in the watchtower than in class.

The problem was that he was barely passing his classes. For the volunteers of school age, good standing in school was a mandatory requirement for continuation in the program. Unfortunately, he couldn't cover the shifts, because of his grades.

Ralph's finger tapped on Betty Finch's name. She could split the watch with Hattie, who was scheduled to come on duty next.

Betty's involvement with the plane spotters. *Perfect.* He had his excuse to speak with Clarinda.

Satisfied that he had found an answer to his problem, Ralph set aside the schedule and finished his lunch in peace.

Now, if only Clarinda would listen.

Chapter 11

Clarinda fidgeted in her seat at the back of the church sanctuary. So much time had passed since she had attended a meeting without leading it, she hardly knew how to act. She didn't even know the exact nature of the meeting, except that it involved a proposal for the women of Maple Notch to support the war effort.

"Settle down, Mom." Anita handed her the notebook she had brought. "Take notes or do something."

Her little girl had grown up, parroting her mother's own words back to her. Clarinda had said it, handing over crayons and coloring book, often enough.

All three girls had decided to attend the meeting with her, after she explained they might be able to work together. She hoped so. As mayor, she felt uncomfortable not participating in a town-wide event.

Aside from Pastor Rucker, only one other man was in attendance—Ralph Quincy. He had taken charge of the entire project, without even explaining the purpose to her. What if she disapproved? She doubted it, not with his involvement.

Clarinda took the notepad Anita had passed to her and wrote *Ralph* in bold letters, underscoring it three times. She couldn't decide if he was making things worse or better. Oh, he wanted to help, she knew that, but the more he helped, the less capable she felt. With three young girls, not to mention all of Maple Notch, depending on her, she couldn't afford to feel helpless. She closed her eyes for a brief prayer. All this worry didn't please God—which only made her worry all the more.

She turned the page and wrote the date at the top of the page when Pastor Rucker walked to the pulpit. He welcomed the ladies to the church, said it was the church's privilege to host the meeting and led an opening prayer before turning the meeting over to Ralph.

Why Ralph was introducing the project instead of herself flummoxed Clarinda. That kind of thing drove Grandma Clara crazy. But Clarinda had promised to keep her hands off this project, and she would keep her word.

Ralph beamed a smile—and what a welcoming, charming smile it was. "Thank you all for joining us today. Last week, one of the plane-spotter volunteers came to me with an idea for another way the ladies of Maple Notch can support the war effort. She asked for my help in getting the word out to the ladies in town, and Pastor Rucker was kind enough to offer the services of the church for us to meet. But since the idea is hers, I will now invite Audrey Smith to the podium."

Audrey? Clarinda clamped her teeth together to keep from staring open jawed. Even if Audrey had a good idea, would she follow through? Clarinda doubted it.

Keep an open mind. You might be surprised. That

was what Ralph had said when he had invited her to the meeting.

She had promised Ralph, and God, when she had prayed about the unknown idea. Clarinda closed her eyes and imagined Grandma Clara behind the podium instead.

When Audrey began speaking, Clarinda opened her eyes to make sure she was listening to the right person. Her lady's suit resembled Clarinda's favorite work outfit—to the point where it looked as though she'd gone to the store and asked if they had another one just like it. She spoke in plain, concise language, clearly at ease. Clarinda wondered if her father-in-law had coached her.

Ralph had warned Clarinda to be prepared for surprises, and he had certainly lived up to the promise.

Audrey held up a newspaper clipping. "I read this in the Boston paper. A women's auxiliary group made a quilt and auctioned it. They raised a substantial sum for the war effort. The mayor complimented the women on their initiative and urged others to think of creative ways to raise money. We've already seen some outstanding examples right here in our community. I see Anita Finch in the back row. Would you stand please?"

Red faced, Anita rose to her feet.

"Although she is only ten years old, Anita led our elementary students in the wonderful circus we enjoyed as part of the New Year's Eve celebration, and they donated all the money to the war effort." Audrey brought her hands together, and soon all the ladies gave her a standing ovation. If Clarinda clapped more loudly than anyone else, who would blame her?

"Why didn't you warn me?" Anita said when at last she was allowed to sit down.

"I didn't know about it," Clarinda said. "A lady should accept a compliment gracefully."

Once the audience was again seated and quiet, Audrey spoke again. "I know that Maple Notch has some of the best quilters in Vermont. How many times have you won at the county fair, Mrs. Hampton?"

"Eight years." Mrs. Hampton's voice rang out.

To give Audrey credit, she knew how to gain her audience's interest.

"But who's counting?" Norma grinned as she whispered to her mother.

"So of course I think we should make a quilt ourselves and hold an auction this summer. Mrs. Rucker is handing out a list with ideas for patriotic quilt designs, and a sign-up sheet is heading down each row. We are hoping that enough of us are interested so that we can make at least two quilts, if not more."

Of course. A quilt representing the history of Maple Notch would be perfect for this project. Someone should have made it long ago. Clarinda's fingers itched to sign up, but she wouldn't, she *couldn't.* Her children must come first.

Anita tugged at her sleeve. "Am I too young to work on a quilt, Mom?"

Ralph had placed his chair where he could keep an eye on the audience in general and on Clarinda in particular. When she bent over to talk with Anita, he wished he could hear them. Did they see the potential in the project? Instead, he prayed.

The meeting ended not long after that. Women gathered in informal circles that he guessed would form the heart of the quilting groups. He passed among them, accepting their well-wishes, as he made his way to the back pew where the Finches were seated.

Anita and Betty leaned in on either side, forming a

tight-knit circle. Norma noticed Ralph and waved him over. "We love the quilt idea, Mr. Quincy! We're going to make one, just the four of us."

Ralph hooked his eyebrow, and Clarinda said, "Anita suggested it, and Norma and Betty love the idea."

"Good. You might be interested to know that Mrs. Smith is giving up the plane-spotter program to head up the quilt project. I think she makes a better queen than a worker bee."

Anita put a hand over her mouth as she giggled.

Ralph simply smiled. "Until later, ladies." He bowed and departed.

Before he could reach his car, however, a female voice called him from the church door. "Hello, Mr. Quincy!"

It was Mrs. Anderson, the former home-economics teacher at the high school. He hadn't made his escape quite soon enough.

"Have you made plans for the girls to do this at school?" she asked in her brightest voice.

"The program wasn't even approved until a few minutes ago."

"I know the girls will want to do their part. Not everyone is cut out to be a plane spotter, but almost everyone can sew."

"Are you volunteering to lead them?" He hoped the current teacher wouldn't object. She could be territorial about her classes.

"Why, I would be honored, Mr. Quincy."

"Why don't you approach Miss Jackson about sponsoring the project together. You do realize, as a former teacher, that they can't spend the entire semester making a quilt."

"But they do study sewing in the second semester. It's the best time of year for the project. I will speak with Miss Jackson about it. I'm sure she'll agree with me."

Ralph expected the teachers would work it out. He would give his approval to the program and make sure the volunteers qualified academically, the same as for any extracurricular activity.

When Ralph arrived at school on Monday, he faced a more critical issue than overseeing the quilt project. Another promising student had left school with no warning. After an evening of excessive celebration of his eighteenth birthday on Friday night, he and another one of the eighteen-year-olds had both staggered into the enlistment office in Burlington on Saturday morning.

"The recruiting officer sent me home straightaway. He didn't believe me when I told him I was of age. I'm eighteen—I know I don't look it, but my birthday was last November. But Everett had proof of his age, and the recruiter signed him up."

Ralph sank wearily into his chair. The same thing had happened to his brother, except it had been Ralph's suggestion, on the morning after his birthday. They had rushed to the enlistment office, had flown through the process and had shipped out soon after. Only one of them came home. All these years later, he still blamed himself.

"I am…saddened that Everett left school so close to graduation, but I am glad that you at least are back. Do you promise to stay until June?"

Leroy shrugged. "I suppose so."

Ralph sat at his desk for a few minutes after Leroy left, thinking hard. He must prepare the seniors—and probably the juniors and perhaps even the sophomores, as well—for service when their time came. With the women taking bigger and bigger roles in the war effort, both at home and abroad, any plans Ralph made had to include all his students. He needed someone to partner with him to prepare the women, and he knew exactly whom to approach.

Clarinda. Should he approach her as the mayor, as the former headmistress of the seminary—or as a friend? Which would she accept? What did he want? It seemed that during a time of war, the young rushed into life, not willing to wait for a tomorrow that might never come. Older people tended to hang back, more aware than ever of the risks involved.

Still uncertain, he called the mayor's office as the high school principal. He reached Hazel and asked for an appointment with the mayor.

"And what may I say is the reason for the appointment?" she asked delicately. Clarinda had probably given her a difficult time after his last unannounced visit.

"I have some ideas to prepare our seniors for the future. I could use her help. I could bring it up at the next council meeting, but I don't think we need an official sanction."

"Very well. Does four o'clock work for you?"

He agreed. He reviewed his tentative plans one final time, then tucked them away in his file folder for the afternoon's visit. Before he left the premises, Mrs. Anderson and Miss Jackson approached him for permission to sponsor the quilt-making project at the high school. He signed off on the proposal and wandered the halls during the last hour, checking on the progress each class was making.

He stopped at one door to observe the French class. Although it was second-year French, Norma Finch had enrolled in the sophomore-level class based on her test scores. She had her hand in the air in response to a question and stood when called upon. Ralph was glad she excelled in most subjects, because she still struggled with algebra.

Seeing Betty a few doors down, in English class, made Ralph think of the youngest Finch child over at the elementary school. From what he had observed, things were going better between mother and daughter.

After finding Clarinda's daughter in the cave, Ralph had crossed the line separating coworker from friend. And he didn't know how Clarinda felt about that.

Clarinda hung up the phone after her discussion with Ralph and swiveled her chair around. She studied Howard's portrait, which had remained there since he had taken office in 1939. Allowing Ralph to make himself a bigger and bigger part of their lives felt disloyal to a man who had given his very life to protect them.

That was then. She swiveled the chair again to face her desk—her future. Did Ralph have a new project for the seniors or was it only an excuse for involving himself once more in her affairs? It didn't matter. She would listen and decide. He had spearheaded the town's plane-spotter program and the quilt project; he might have another brilliant idea.

When Clarinda spotted Ralph on the town square, she walked to the window. His dark hair with its distinguished-looking gray sideburns refused to stay in the controlled style he preferred, especially not when a breeze teased it into waves. He cut a fine figure, handsome, distinguished, his ever-present briefcase in his left hand.

When he turned onto the sidewalk leading to the town hall, Clarinda sat behind her desk and opened her date book. At last, her attempts to lessen her appointments were taking hold. She had delegated several committees to various council members instead of her personal supervision. Hazel helped her minimize the amount of paperwork, so Clarinda found herself with more time with her girls. Every spare minute, they worked on the quilt project after the homework was done.

The intercom rang, and Hazel announced that Mr.

Quincy had arrived. "Send him in," Clarinda said. She adjusted the scarf around her neck as he walked in.

"Good afternoon, Clarinda. Thank you for agreeing to see me on such short notice."

"Let's get to business. I leave right at five these days, except for emergencies."

He shook his head. "No emergency today. I only wanted to run an idea by you. I don't think this requires the council's approval, but I would welcome your support before I start."

"I'm listening." Clarinda reminded herself that Ralph was a competent politician. She'd bring the matter before the council if necessary.

When Ralph mentioned the departure of another senior into the service, Clarinda felt grief stab her own heart. Did a few months make that much of a difference, one way or another? If Arthur could jump into the navy before he had finished college… *Listen.* She wrenched her attention back to Ralph.

"Our students need to see the relevance of their education to war. I also believe they should know the range of service opportunities available to both men and women. Male or female, 4-F status or a good candidate, everyone can make a difference. We need people to present seminars to our students."

Clarinda leaned forward. Yes, the women should know their choices. Factory work was far from the only arena where they could make a difference.

"I know they all respect you—a woman mayor is still a rarity. I would love for you to spearhead that training."

Clarinda narrowed her eyes and tapped the blotter with her pen. "I don't know much about women in the service, although I do like your idea. Surely one of your teachers could lead the class just as well as I could." She stared at him without blinking as if daring him to disagree.

His decision to stop by the recruiting office before speaking with Clarinda had turned into a wise decision. "Here is information on the women's auxiliary services to the different branches of service. They should give you a good start. The officer at the recruiting office also volunteered to come out and speak."

Ralph didn't blame Clarinda for her mutinous expression. After all, he was the one who had encouraged her to cut back on her extracurricular activities, and here he was contradicting his advice by asking for her help.

The ace up his sleeve should convince her. "There is something else you should know."

"Yes?" Clarinda raised one carefully plucked eyebrow.

Ralph considered again whether he should reveal what he knew. No one had sworn him to secrecy. "A couple of seniors went to the recruiting office with me."

The polite expression on her face told him she didn't yet understand.

"We went shortly after you were ready to stop Betty's participation in the plane-spotter program, after Audrey had the problem driving during the blackout."

Clarinda's mouth formed a small O.

"Betty came with me. She's ready to bolt. If you don't guide her, and our other girls, they may end up making the worst choices of their lives."

Chapter 12

The day after Valentine's Day, Clarinda gathered with the girls for the Finch family night. They hadn't missed a Monday yet, and in between, they headed for the back room they had converted into a sewing room whenever they had a few spare moments. They had finished cutting the pieces needed for the complicated quilt pattern Clarinda's brother, Wallace, had helped them create.

At first the girls had sniffed at making a quilt celebrating the history of Maple Notch. That disappointed Clarinda, but as other groups announced their themes, the girls decided they liked the unique nature of Clarinda's idea. Most groups were making a flag-themed pattern in red, white and blue; another group chose the difficult pattern of the insignias for all the branches of military service.

When Clarinda arrived home, she followed the sound of girlish laughter to the back room, expecting to find at least two of them hard at work on the quilt.

All three girls were present, but no one was quilting. They had found the pictures of women in uniform that Clarinda had gathered to use in her workshop.

Norma had draped a length of olive-colored material over her shoulder. "What do you think, ladies? Does this color suit me, or should I go with navy blue?" She exchanged the olive for a different swatch of cloth.

Anita had folded a newspaper into a nurse's cap and placed it on her head. She draped navy blue fabric over her shoulders like a cape and swirled around, sending the fabric flying. When she spotted Clarinda, her eyes widened, and she stopped. "Hi, Mom."

"So you want to be a nurse?" Clarinda fought to keep her tone light. *Please, God, let this war be over long before Anita or even Norma are old enough to enlist.*

"Actually, I'd like to be a doctor, but they only take women as nurses." Anita sounded perplexed, and Clarinda rejoiced that she might dream of medical school.

"You can still become a doctor," Clarinda said. "Or anything else you dream about. You have plenty of time to make up your mind."

Betty shuffled through the pages, picking up first one, then another. "I'm the one running out of time. But I'm pretty sure I know which branch of the service I want to join."

"You could always serve the war effort in other ways, without even leaving Maple Notch. I am." The words came out before Clarinda could stop them.

Betty frowned.

"But of course, whatever branch of the service you choose to join will be lucky to have you." Clarinda looked through the picture samples the girls had assembled. The portraits featured bright, beautiful, dedicated young women.

Who wouldn't want to be like them? At least Betty was thinking about more than how she would look.

That was the problem. She'd probably choose the branch with the greatest need—where she'd encounter the greatest danger.

"We've got examples from every women's group. I'll have Hazel put the pictures with the pamphlets in a notebook, so girls can examine at leisure." Clarinda put the pages in a manila folder and set it on a side counter. "Now, where are we with the quilt?"

The various quilting groups had proposed an additional incentive for finishing their projects. The group that finished first would receive a $50 gift certificate for more fabric from the local store. The first five groups to finish would also receive certificates, decreasing by ten dollars for each place.

Clarinda didn't expect to finish first, but they might make the top five. However, with only four of them, and the difficulty of the project… "We'll just have to work harder."

Anita looked puzzled, but Betty laughed. "You jumped about five steps ahead of us. I'd love to beat out the high school group at least. Do you mind if I start piecing the river together?"

The Bumblebee River ran through the design from the upper right-hand corner to the lower left-hand corner, with a covered bridge in one of the squares. Since it crossed over and between squares, Betty had chosen the most difficult part of the quilt as her own.

"Of course. Anita and I can start with the cave, unless you want to help her with it, Norma?"

Norma opened her mouth to speak when the phone rang. She jumped out of her chair and disappeared out the door. Anita looked at Betty, who shook her head.

Betty had spent a lot of time on the phone when she had started high school, Clarinda remembered. In fact, Betty still did. Since Clarinda had become mayor, Clarinda had enforced a five-minute rule. People needed access to the mayor at any time of the day or night. She committed the time on her watch to memory before she turned to Anita. "Let's get the pieces we need for the cave."

Anita grinned. "I'm glad I get to sew the cave." She tugged together several pieces of gray cloth toward her and pieced them into the shape of the interior walls of the cave. "I can't imagine a family living in there for months, like our ancestors did. It's dark and cold and smelly."

Maybe Anita's recent escapade had cured her of romanticizing.

"The father of their family died in the battle at Fort Ticonderoga." Clarinda never missed a chance to remind them of the family history.

"Like Daddy did in the war?" Anita asked.

Clarinda nodded. "And they were in danger of losing their farm. The same land where we have a house today." She glanced at her watch—ten seconds left.

The door opened, and Norma came back in. Her face flushed, she asked, "May I go with some friends to see a movie in Burlington on Saturday night?"

Ralph liked to roam the school halls during the pass period. He learned as much about the pulse of the school through the snippets of conversation he heard as he did from any teacher reports.

This time of year students were often restless. Only one week remained until spring break, although winter still held Vermont in its grasp well into March. When students' thoughts turned to love, spring fever infected them like a virus.

Today was a good example of the phenomenon. While he wandered down the hall, he ran into Betty Finch chatting with one of the boys—in French. The two of them raced each other for the title of class valedictorian.

What the pair might not know was that Ralph spoke fluent French. The boy was asking Betty out to dinner on Thursday night.

Betty shook her head. "Mom only lets me go out on the weekend."

The boy persisted. How about Friday night, then? She was working her shift as a plane spotter. Saturday? She was babysitting the workers' children.

Poor Steve was about to give up, but Ralph sensed Betty's frustration. No senior girl should be so busy that she couldn't go on a date. Grinning to himself, Ralph joined the stream of traffic and "accidentally" ran across the couple. "Miss Finch, I'm so glad I ran into you. Mrs. Charles asked if she could switch shifts with you. She's scheduled for Thursday night."

Betty's eyes lit up. "I'll check with Mom, but I'm sure she'll say it's okay."

Ralph wasn't so sure—Clarinda had asked that Betty not work on weeknights. The undercurrent of the French conversation as he left them behind put a smile on Ralph's face. Well done, Steve. He and Betty made a good match. If Clarinda had any sense, she'd see it, too.

The bell rang for the next period, and Ralph waited in the stairwell as the halls cleared. As the noisy ringing ended, he headed back to his office. At the same time, heels *tat-a-tatt*ed on the stairs, and he nearly ran into Norma Finch.

"Oh, Mr. Quincy. Excuse me. I'm sorry."

Ralph glanced at his watch, although Norma knew as well as he did that the next class had started. "You are late for class. And I believe this is the period your algebra class meets, isn't it?"

"Yes, sir." She hesitated. "May I go, sir?"

"Go on." Ralph held the door open for her as she quick-stepped into the hallway. Before he could follow, he heard whistling coming from the upper floor—George Walker. Ralph would bet his bottom dollar that George had everything to do with Norma being late to class.

Ralph shut the door so that George would think he had gone and then waited. When the boy barreled through the door a minute later, he almost ran into the principal.

"I gotta get to world history, Mr. Quincy."

"I'll walk with you to your classroom." They passed the cafeteria before either one of them spoke.

"You won't tell Mrs. Finch about me and Norma, will you?"

How many times had Ralph heard a similar request from a young man? Not so many years ago, the mayor's son had asked the same thing while he was courting Audrey. Ralph shook his head. "Not unless either one of you give me reason to. Like being late for class." He let the warning sink in. "But it will be best if you let Mrs. Finch know that you are interested in her daughter. I'll tell you one thing about our mayor—she doesn't like surprises."

George laughed nervously. "She knows we go out in a group and doesn't mind."

Ralph doubted it would end there. George would want a one-on-one date with the charming young Miss Finch. And Ralph didn't know if Clarinda was ready for that. Everywhere she turned, things were changing. In this environment, her family's 150 years of tradition made moving forward difficult.

Shaking his head, Ralph headed back to his office. Some parents said he couldn't understand, since he didn't have any children himself. But he had taught plenty of them over the years, and he knew a few tricks parents didn't.

At lunchtime, he headed to the town hall. He had convinced Clarinda to turn a few routine jobs over to her secretary. He still hoped to persuade her to pass even more duties over to the members of the council.

When he reached the mayor's office, Hazel greeted him. "She's expecting you, so go ahead in."

He looked around the office, noting more of the changes Clarinda had made to the room from since before Bill Smith's tenure. Photographs and sketches of Maple Notch past and present covered warm beige walls. Behind her hung a picture of Howard Finch, who'd been mayor for three years. Overall, the room held more than it had while Smith was mayor, but it was so well organized that it didn't feel cluttered.

How did a woman who was so organized cope with the clutter that accumulated when a large group of people lived together?

Today she wore a claret-red blouse with a black skirt, which suited her coloring, reflecting her usual good taste. "Take a seat, Ralph." She had placed a plate and napkins on either side of the desk. Hazel came in with two cups of coffee.

"You don't have to go to all this trouble." Ralph rarely set a table with good china, even for Sunday dinners.

"It's my pleasure." A gentle pink colored her cheeks.

He circled the desk and held her seat for her. After she settled in, she draped her napkin over her skirt.

He left his napkin beside his plate, placing two ham sandwiches, an apple and a couple of cookies on the dish. He tasted the coffee. "Good, as always. Hazel can make coffee for me anytime."

"Flattery will get you anywhere, Mr. Quincy." Hazel winked and left, leaving the door partially open. Closed-door sessions would get the town rumor mill started faster than spotting a plane overhead. He grinned at the analogy.

"What are you smiling at?" Clarinda asked.

Ralph wouldn't talk about the rumor mill. She'd stop their lunch meetings. "Wondering what will happen if one of our volunteers actually spots an enemy plane."

She arched an eyebrow. "That's all included in the training."

"Of course." He waved his hand as if it didn't matter. "I have no doubt that the spotter would make the necessary phone calls. But how prepared are we, as a town, to deal with the possibility? Are we any more prepared than the folks at Pearl Harbor were?"

"Then why do we bother looking for planes at all, if you don't think it will make a difference?" She frowned at her soup, which she had poured into the thermos cup. She sounded more curious than ready to stop the program.

"Some warning is better than none. If we see them here and pass on the word to the bigger cities down south of us, they can do more to get ready."

"National implications. I see." She dipped a spoon into the soup and smiled.

Clarinda had come to look forward to her daily lunches with Ralph, although she wouldn't admit it to anyone. Today was different, however. Even should he announce his candidacy for the governor of Vermont, she wouldn't pay attention.

Arthur was coming home from basic training today. After a brief twenty-six hours, he had to return to base and ship out. She didn't know whether to laugh or cry, and guessed she might do both.

Ralph was in the middle of describing another idea for the war effort, but Clarinda listened with only half an ear. Out the window, she spotted her girls scurrying across the town square in the direction of the town hall. She started to rise from her chair, then realized Ralph was still talking.

He followed the direction of her gaze. "What are the girls doing out of school at one o'clock?"

"You don't follow the excused absences?" Clarinda asked. That answered the question of why he hadn't asked after Arthur.

Ralph shook his head. "Not unless my secretary senses something odd about the request or in cases of a family emergency." He didn't put his question into words, but she could read it in his eyes.

"No emergency." She bit her lip. "Arthur is coming home from basic training. Friends are supposed to drop him off here at the town hall in thirty minutes and pick him up tomorrow afternoon." She couldn't help it. Tears scalded her voice.

In answer, Ralph cleared both their plates. "I won't expect to see you tomorrow, then. Go ahead and enjoy your time with your son."

She thought she said thank-you, but she wasn't sure as the door closed behind him. After a couple of minutes, she roused herself enough to ask Hazel to brew some fresh coffee. The girls came in while Clarinda approved a final purchase order to conclude her business for the day.

"Mr. Quincy caught us sneaking in." Norma spoke as if their plans were a secret mission. "I don't understand why we couldn't meet Arthur at the house."

Betty laughed. "That's easy! He wouldn't get any peace over there. All the single women would flirt with him." She winked at Clarinda when she said this. "This time belongs to the five of us. If only Howie were here…"

Clarinda reached into the top drawer of her desk. "Here's the next best thing. We received a letter from him today."

The three girls swarmed the desk, three arms reaching around Clarinda while she held the envelope over her head. "Settle down."

Her "Aunt Flo voice" worked as it always did. "I will read you the letter." He told a lot of humorous accounts of life among the soldiers. News of the battles was forbidden, but Howie made it sound as though he was at summer camp.

The plan worked as well as Clarinda had hoped it would, the three of them so interested in Howie's news that they didn't keep running to the window. Her eyes kept straying in that direction, however, and a tiny yelp escaped from her lips when she spotted a pair of olive-green-covered legs swing out the car door.

"He's here!" Betty ran to the window.

They left by the Emergency Only exit. Anita reached Arthur first, throwing herself into his arms. Norma ran a few feet, then slowed. Betty strode with the confident steps of a young woman. Soon all four of her children were gathered in a tight embrace. Clarinda stood on the edge, watching them, thanking God that all five of her children were alive and healthy, as of the time Howie wrote his last letter. Having four of them together at the same time was a rare blessing in this day and age.

"Hi, Mom." Arthur stood straight and tall, as if he had matured five years instead of three months. "I'm afraid I have bad news. We need to pull out tomorrow morning, not in the afternoon."

Clarinda swallowed past the lump in her throat. "Thank you for telling us. Let's get going." She linked her arm with his and headed for the parking lot. "I drove the car today to sneak you in by a back door, so we can visit without every girl in the building taking your time."

"If it isn't Arthur Finch," Rusty Henshaw called as he ran across the road. "Smile for the camera."

Chapter 13

Ralph would never tell Clarinda because she might never forgive him, but the reporter's appearance on the town square was his fault. After he'd left town hall, he ran into Rusty at the store.

"What's up with you and Mayor Finch?" Rusty asked the question as if he had a right to know.

"Nothing. Her son Arthur is coming from basic training any minute now."

"Why didn't you say so?" Ralph dashed out of the store.

Rich put his purchases to the side. "He'll be back. He's done this before." He leaned across the counter. "So what *is* going on between you and the magisterial Mrs. Finch?"

Ralph grunted. *Magisterial* didn't fit Clarinda—commanding, regal, beautiful, even. But if he corrected his friend's compliment, he would only make matters worse. "I'd better get back to the office. See you later."

He exited the store in time to see Rusty catch Clarinda

and Arthur unaware. The picture would become a classic, he suspected, the pride, joy and happiness on Clarinda's face, the shy pride in the jut of Arthur's jaw, his strut. Clarinda wouldn't like it, though. She would insist that she wasn't doing anything more than the rest of America, that she was nothing special. She would refuse to recognize the inspiration she could be, the way she represented America at its best.

At least he didn't have to face her displeasure over lunch tomorrow. She would spend her lunch hour with Arthur. Not seeing her again until Wednesday noon loomed like a long time. Maybe he'd catch up on some of the latest six-week report cards, review those students who were in trouble. See if Norma Finch's math grades had improved so he could give Clarinda an update.

The next morning, Ralph reverted to his old habits, not grooming with the care he took when meeting with Clarinda. His secretary had already stacked messages on his desk when he came in. The top message came from Clarinda. Curiosity piqued, he lifted the receiver from the phone and dialed the number—her *office* number.

After Hazel put his call through, he asked, "What are you doing in the office this morning? I expected you to enjoy a leisurely morning with Arthur."

She didn't answer for a few seconds. "He had to leave this morning. The girls went to school, and the house felt empty."

Poor Clarinda.

"I know you have been working advertising for the quilt auction. I wonder if you would be willing to give up your lunch hour today to discuss your plans?"

Ralph could have cheered. At a time when Clarinda felt sad, she had asked him for a lunch date—for the first time. She had reached out to him. He wanted to rush right over now, as soon as the first bell sounded. Instead, he said, "Of course. Although I'll be poor company compared to Arthur."

"Not worse company. *Different*." She sounded a little relieved.

Ralph relaxed. "I'll see you later, then."

During the last period before lunch, Ralph took a call from Mrs. Wilson, the elementary school principal. "Ralph, thank you for calling back." They exchanged a few pleasantries, before she got to the reason for her phone call. "I don't mean to pry, but I understand there was an… incident…with Anita Finch a couple of months back, and that you were involved."

Ralph's mind raced. Should he talk with Clarinda before he betrayed any personal information? Not necessarily. "Why are you asking? Is she in some kind of trouble?"

"She skipped a class this morning. It's not a big thing, but it's unlike her," Mrs. Wilson said.

"Her brother Arthur came home for a brief leave last night." Ralph tapped his pencil on the pad. "Betty and Norma had excused absences for the day."

"That explains it." They updated each other on a few students and said goodbye.

After he replaced the receiver, Ralph studied his daily planner. In spite of his dismissive words to Mrs. Wilson, he suspected that more was involved in Anita's absence than bidding Arthur farewell.

Should he tell Clarinda about Anita's brief truancy? She of course would expect to be told. He would wait until his lunch meeting with Clarinda, no longer.

"I may not make it back before the meeting with the math teachers today." He would have to catch up on Norma's progress later. Grabbing his coat, he reached the exit as the lunch bell sounded, releasing the hungry students speeding toward the cafeteria.

He drove to the town hall, in case he needed the car to hunt for Anita. When he arrived at Clarinda's office, Hazel looked up, smiling. "You're here early."

He shrugged. "I finished up business this morning a little early." He knocked on the door to Clarinda's office and entered.

The happy look on Clarinda's face made Ralph wish he had anything on his mind beyond Anita's puzzling absence from class. Something that involved him and Clarinda on a drive through spring's twilight.

When Clarinda had said goodbye to Arthur that morning, she had surprised herself more than anyone else by wanting to talk to Ralph about their visit, as brief as it was. She knew she was smiling, but today she didn't care.

Rather than answering her smile, Ralph looked less than pleased.

"I hope I didn't pull you away from something important." She continued smiling while her heart sped up its beat.

"No." He settled into his chair and arranged his meal on the plate in front of him. Today he had a slice of ham and some leftover corn bread.

Clarinda glanced at his plate before pulling out her own chicken salad. "You must let me prepare you an honest-to-goodness home-cooked meal one of these days."

"I would like that."

A new picture of Arthur in uniform stood on top of her filing cabinet, together with a card. "What's the occasion?" Ralph pointed to the card next to the picture.

"Oh, it's an early birthday card. He got me this card

with a lovely picture and a sentimental verse. 'While we're apart.'" She stopped speaking before she began to cry.

A memory tickled Ralph's mind. "You and my brother have the same birthday."

"How do you know my birthday?" She didn't know his.

He laughed. "It stems from attending church together all our lives. They always celebrated your birthdays at the same time."

"I remember." She closed her mouth. *Ralph's brother, Johnny.* "Until the year we both turned eighteen. Your family received a telegram instead of sending a birthday card."

The color fled Ralph's face. "He wasn't even eighteen yet. He had convinced that recruiting officer that he was old enough, and they were glad enough to send him."

"Oh, Ralph." Without thought, Clarinda rose from her chair and rounded the desk before laying a hand on his shoulder. "No wonder you don't want any of our boys rushing into battle before their time."

"I pray for them like they were my own sons every night. And thank God for every day that goes by without a telegram arriving at someone's door."

"I do, as well." Clarinda stood there for another minute, their breaths joining, intake and exhale like a prayer.

They were still standing like that when the door popped open, and Anita ran in. "Mr. Quincy!"

Clarinda jerked her hand away from Ralph's shoulder and stepped back to her chair. "Anita. I didn't expect to see you here."

"I asked if I could come over here during lunch. They said yes." Her lower lip trembled a little bit.

Ralph stood. "I'll be going, then. Same time tomorrow, Mayor?"

Clarinda nodded. "We'll discuss the auction tomorrow."

"Of course." Was it just her imagination, or did he look disappointed?

Anita took the seat Ralph had vacated, her ever-lengthening legs *tap-tap-tap*ping against the floor.

"Do you have your lunch with you?" Clarinda asked. "Or did you already eat?"

"I ate most of it at recess time." Anita looked out the window, away from her mother's face. "I was hungry."

Anita's dispirited answer poked a hole in the joyful bubble that had encompassed Clarinda since Arthur's brief visit. Of all of them, Anita had had the hardest time saying goodbye. She wouldn't even leave her room when he left that morning.

Arthur had said it didn't matter, but he couldn't hide his hurt from a mother's eyes. "Take care of Norma and Anita, Mom. Betty's going to be fine...."

"Don't worry about us. When you think of Maple Notch, imagine—" Imagine what? Life as it had been before the war started was impossible. Howard was dead, and both sons fought in the war. With Betty poised to graduate, Norma and Anita growing up, the family life Arthur returned to would be nothing like the family he left behind.

By the time he returned, he might have a family of his own. The thought brought tears to Clarinda's eyes, and she turned away from Anita long enough to run a handkerchief across her face. "Let me share some of my lunch with you." She split the still uneaten chicken salad sandwich in half and poured a glass of milk from a bottle they kept in the refrigerator. With a brief thought to the cookies she had promised herself, she gave them both to Anita, and took an apple from the cooler for herself.

"Thanks, Mom." Anita scarfed down one cookie before starting on the sandwich. She glanced at the clock and relaxed. In a few minutes, she had to return to school.

Anita did not speak; the only sound she made was the tapping of her foot on the floor. Clarinda wanted to ask why her youngest joined her for lunch today, although she could guess. A direct inquiry wouldn't receive a satisfactory answer, she knew from experience.

When Anita at last spoke, she didn't mention Arthur. "Mom, are you dating Mr. Quincy?"

Ralph intended to return straight to the school, but his shoe caught a stone in the path and it bounced in the air. He leaned over and picked it up, rubbing the surface worn smooth by the years of harsh New England winters. It would make a nice addition to his rock collection.

He tossed it in the air and caught it again. He picked a park bench to wait.

A few minutes later, Anita ran down the front steps of town hall. Ralph left the quiet of town square and caught up with her on the sidewalk. "Hello there, Anita."

She stopped. "Mr. Quincy, I'll be late getting back to school."

"Don't worry. I'll take care of Mrs. Wilson. Do you mind if I walk back with you?"

"No." Her slumped shoulders said that she lied.

Ralph decided to walk with her anyhow. "I know about this morning."

Anita's eyes widened.

"Don't worry. I didn't tell your mother." *I didn't have a chance.*

"Why not? You see each other all the time. Kids at school ask me if you're getting married." Anita kept her gaze trained forward, but he saw her frown.

His ears grew warm, but Ralph kept his voice level. "Your mother is a good friend and an even better mayor. I only want to help her do her best job." *Now who's lying?*

Her shoulders relaxed a little bit. "Good."

They walked in silence for a minute or so before Ralph spoke again. "Do you collect anything?"

Anita squinted her eyes at the question. "I like to collect stamps. I don't have very many, though."

"Well, I started a rock collection when I was a boy. And I still have it."

"Are any of them valuable?" Anita asked.

A reasonable question. "Not that I know of. I keep them because they mean something special to me. Either I think they're pretty, or I found them when I was doing something else that I wanted to remember."

"You sound like Uncle Walter and his birds." Anita sounded amused.

"What do you think of this one?" He pulled out the stone he had found outside the town hall.

She took it in her hand, feeling its weight, rubbing her thumb over its almost granite smoothness, tossing it up into the air and then catching it again. She held it out. "It's a nice rock."

He nodded. "But I already have one a lot like it. In fact, I have it in my pocket right now." He dug in his left pocket and pulled out a stone that could have been a twin to the one in Anita's hand.

She compared them side by side. "What's so special about these rocks?"

Ralph searched for the right words to express what was in his heart. "You know that the United States fought in the Great War before you were born."

Anita nodded.

"Both my brother and I joined the army. He never came home. He's buried over there, in Belgium."

Anita stopped walking. "I'm sorry." She began walking again. "Does it get easier? The more that time goes by? That's what everyone keeps saying."

"I won't lie and pretend everything gets better. You'll always miss your dad. But it does get easier. I haven't cried over Johnny for years, and then this year I've thought of him all the time."

Anita handed the stone back to him. "So what does the stone have to do with your brother?"

"Pastor Rucker knew I collected rocks, and he gave it to me. Told me whenever I felt sad or mad, I could feel the rock in my pocket and remember that God loves me. That I could talk to Him about anything." Even as he was speaking, he ran his fingers over the smooth surface.

Anita smiled.

"You keep that rock. Maybe you can carry it in your purse in case your dress doesn't have pockets," Ralph said. "Your father isn't here, and your mother can't be with you all the time, but God is. You might even want to paint the rock."

"Like with a rainbow."

"Or a word, like *God* or *love*."

Anita flipped the rock over, nodded and slipped it into her coat pocket. "Thank you, Mr. Quincy." She nodded, as if that settled it.

"Does this mean we're friends?" Ralph asked.

"I s'pose." Anita glanced at him, with a shy smile.

"Good. Because I need a friend's help to plan something special. You know your mother's birthday is next week…"

Ralph usually sampled his cooking before serving it to others, in case he did something disastrous like substitute salt for sugar. But if he did that with the cake, he'd ruin it. Instead, he double-checked every step of a recipe he'd made a hundred times before.

The process took longer than he had expected, and he was late leaving for the first town-council meeting in April. The phone rang. "She just left. She doesn't suspect a thing."

"Hazel will get you when it's time." Ralph unlocked his front door. "I'm on my way."

Unlike his usual practice, Ralph parked at the side of the parking lot hidden from the mayor's office and the conference room. The side door was unlocked, as Hazel had promised. She waited in the small kitchen for the coffee to finish brewing. Lifting the corner of the towel covering Ralph's cake pan, she smiled. "It's beautiful."

"You have everything else?" His most important contribution to the evening waited inside his briefcase.

Hazel nodded. "Come with me as I walk to the conference room."

As Ralph had expected, he arrived at the council meeting after everyone else. Today's meeting only covered an expected amicable discussion about the upcoming quilt auction, easily tabled in light of the true purpose of tonight's meeting. He allowed himself a small grin.

Clarinda quickly dispatched of the opening prayer and Pledge of Allegiance before Hazel knocked at the door. Ralph jumped to answer it, to make it easier for her to enter.

Birthday candles flamed on the surface of the chocolate-frosted cake. Cheers of "happy birthday" rang from every corner of the room.

Chapter 14

In the secret places of Clarinda's heart, the fuss at the council meeting pleased her, but she felt as though she should protest. "Town-council meetings aren't the place for birthday celebrations."

Ralph grinned. "We finished the meeting five minutes ago."

More heat sprang into Clarinda's cheeks at his comment. For someone who usually spent the day mourning his brother's death, Ralph seemed chipper. "A little bird reminded me of the day, and I offered to bring the cake. I figured I had the most ration coupons to spare, since I only have to feed myself." He grinned, his teeth whiter than a man approaching fifty should have.

Clarinda looked at Betty first, expecting her to turn a guilty red. Instead, Anita clapped her hands together. "Blow the candles out before they burn up the cake," she said.

Candles circled the center of the cake. Clarinda drew a deep breath.

"Make a wish." Norma's grin matched Anita's. Clarinda's thoughts flew to Ralph as she blew out the candles.

"Ah, shucks, you missed one. You won't get your wish." Norma didn't sound too upset.

Clarinda looked around the room, at her faithful secretary, fellow council members, her dear children. "I already have more than I could ever wish for."

"Not even—" Ralph reached behind his back "—presents?"

She stared at the gaily decorated package in his hands, the bow tied with military precision. "What's this?"

Ralph looked a little shy. "It's your birthday present. Go ahead, open it."

Clarinda looked at Ralph with a smile. "It's a rectangle, but not a book." She slipped her fingernail under the paper and touched a cool surface. A picture, perhaps. She pulled away the paper and gasped.

Ralph's grin showed her pleasure made him happy. "I found an old photograph in the school files. I was going to give it to you, then I thought, why not see what wonders Rusty might be able to do with his fancy equipment."

Clarinda turned the framed photograph around so the others could see. "It's the Bailey Mansion ten years before it was turned into the seminary."

Murmurs of appreciation passed through the council. Betty took the photograph next and admired it. "This is so good, Mom. You'll have to hang it in the entryway."

After the picture went around the group, Clarinda wrapped it carefully in the original paper. "Thank you, Ralph. I can't think of anything I would like more."

A few minutes later, the party broke up, and she walked home with the girls.

"I know it's late," Anita said. "But I didn't think you would mind."

Clarinda shook her head with a smile.

"I bet you thought we weren't doing anything for your birthday," Norma said.

Clarinda didn't care to admit exactly what she had thought. With the world at war, what did one person's birthday matter? "The cake was perfect. Tonight was a surprise."

To think Ralph was behind it all, giving of his rationing coupons and fixing the photograph. No one had shown such kindness to her since Howard's death. The feelings for Ralph she had pushed aside for days, weeks, even months, made their way around and over the wall she had erected to protect her heart. When she closed her eyes to bring Howard to mind, she saw Ralph's features instead.

Three weeks later, Clarinda clung to the happy memories of her birthday. A defiant Anita stood across from her, a basket of colored Easter eggs between them.

"I helped you color the Easter eggs, but I'm not going on the egg hunt. I'm not a child anymore." She pulled her lips into an ugly mask. "I didn't hunt for eggs last year, and I'm not going to this year, either." She stomped her foot and ran out the door.

Clarinda sat down and held her head with her hands. Her hopes that the Easter-egg tradition would ease memories of last year had proved unwise. Didn't Anita know how hard it was for her to celebrate Easter, herself? To make new dresses and boil eggs and plan an Easter-egg hunt for the town?

The telegram about Howard had been delivered to the mayor's office on Good Friday 1942. Clarinda didn't know if she would ever enjoy the holiday again. The past few weeks had awakened a lot of memories, although she held them in. This morning was the hardest of all. She wanted to go to bed and sleep so she wouldn't have to remember the pain.

Instead she would walk across the street to the town square. Not far at all, in physical distance. She touched her dress, which she had made in hopes of welcoming Howard home last year.

She should have worn something different. If she rushed, she had time to change.

No. She wouldn't give in to her sadness. Why, this was the weekend when Christians across the world celebrated new life in Christ, life after death for those who believed. She would see Howard again someday.

She wrapped her arms around her chest. That truth didn't help when she longed for someone to hold her at night.

Norma came in, cutting off Clarinda's melancholy. "What can I do to help?"

Clarinda noticed the bit of bright red color on her lips. The thought of chastising Norma for wearing lipstick passed quickly. Norma probably wanted to attract George Walker's attention. They thought Clarinda was clueless about their so-called dates, but George's mother had given her all the details.

"Betty's not coming." Norma shrugged.

"I told her to sleep in. She was up late last night with the children, and she'll be up bright and early tomorrow for the sunrise service."

Norma put on a cardigan—young enough to not find the April air chilly—and grabbed the large basket with brightly colored eggs. "Where is Anita?"

"She's not coming. Thinks she's too old for the hunt."

"That's too bad." Norma shrugged as if she wasn't surprised. "I kept going to the hunt to 'help Anita' because I loved the special treats we got afterward."

Clarinda's mind flew to the baskets she had filled with goodies, one for her girls and smaller ones for the residents' children. Last year she could have eaten all of the candy herself, since they killed her pain for a little while. Before long, she'd discovered her clothes didn't fit as well as before, and she'd cut back. She patted her dress as a reminder.

When they left the house, Clarinda sought out Ralph. He stood with a gaggle of girls around him, tossing jelly beans into the air—at least she guessed they were jelly beans, such small, colorful things—for the children's eager hands. When he looked up, he smiled and waved them over.

Rusty was present already, snapping pictures. He took one of Clarinda and Norma as they crossed the street.

"You're here bright and early," Clarinda said.

Rusty nodded. "Pictures of children sell papers. Parents buy copies to give to everyone they know."

Clarinda handed her basket of eggs to Audrey Smith, who had volunteered to help. As she took them, Audrey said, "I didn't expect so many children to be here so early. Will you help Mr. Quincy keep them distracted while we hide the eggs?"

"Of course. Norma, do you want to come with me or to help hide the eggs?"

"Oh, hide the eggs." Norma grinned. "I know all the best hiding places."

Clarinda crossed the grass with quick steps, eager to see Ralph. How could she cry over Howard and look forward to seeing another man, both at the same time? She almost felt guilty. *This is just the annual town Easter-egg hunt. Nothing more than that.*

She watched Ralph play with the children until they

came to a short break. "Audrey asked me to help you keep the children distracted, but you seem to be doing fine all by yourself."

Ralph held up a half-empty bag of jelly beans. "The problem is, the more candy they eat, the faster they run around."

"Toss one to me!" Joey, one of the boys who lived in the dormitory, said. Ralph complied.

"Maybe we can try a game," Clarinda suggested. "How about Simon Says?"

"We want more jelly beans," Joey's sister Mandy said.

"Later. You can be Simon first, though."

The children created a straggling line.

"Simon says clap your hands." Mandy caught a couple of the children unprepared, and she frowned.

"Speak up this time. You might need to shout," Clarinda said.

"Simon says stomp your feet." Mandy shouted so loud that Audrey looked up.

Every child stomped his foot.

With the next command, Mandy didn't say "Simon says." She caught her brother Joey, and he had to take her place.

After a few turns, Ralph took over, leading them in a game of red light, green light. Mrs. Rucker came out of the church basement. "We're all ready when the hunt is over. I'll let Mrs. Smith know."

A few minutes later, Audrey blew a whistle. "We're ready!" The kids left the game without a thought and pelted in her direction.

Ralph and Clarinda followed at a slower pace. "I haven't supervised children in games like that since I had to supervise recess." He tossed a softball in the air and caught it. "I forgot how they wear you out."

"The girls at the seminary played organized games. Aunt Flo used to say it kept her young." *Oh, Aunt Flo.*

"You played on a championship softball team, if I remember correctly." Ralph tossed the ball at her.

Clarinda caught it with a small laugh. "That was how I met Howard. He was so crazy about baseball, he'd even come to watch the girls play."

Ralph kept quiet for several minutes, and Clarinda wondered if mentioning Howard had erected a barrier between them.

"I wondered if you would come today," Ralph said. "I couldn't face Easter for years after my brother died." Ralph gestured at the children gathered in front of them. "I don't see Anita. She's not eleven yet, is she?"

Clarinda shook her head. "Her birthday is in October, so she's still young enough to take part. But she felt it was too childish." Clarinda tugged her coat around her as a chill went through her. "In some ways, her childhood ended last Easter. And there is nothing I can do to change that."

"Except love her and be there for her. You're only human, Clarinda, but I think you've done a difficult job with grace and courage."

Howard. As always, everything Ralph did with Clarinda circled to her husband sooner or later. How could he compete with a war hero?

He couldn't. He shouldn't try to. If he ever decided to actively pursue Clarinda—a thought that pressed on his mind more and more—he had to do it on his own terms, not as a substitute for another man.

At least this year she had joined the Easter celebration. He took this as a good sign that she was moving forward out of her grief.

Anita was another story. Ever since Ralph had given her

the prayer stone, she had acted friendly enough, and now it sounded as if she needed him again. Did he have any wisdom to share? Maybe all she needed was a listening ear.

Satisfied that the egg hunt could continue without him, Ralph took off for the church parking lot, where his car waited. A large area behind the church housed young green plants pushing up through the soil. Even the church was patriotic these days, members using the extra space for a victory garden instead of an occasional baseball game. The plot at the high school suffered from too much attention. The plants would either flourish from all the love or die from overwatering.

The plants could die. The words rumbled through Ralph's brain, and an idea grew in his mind. By Wednesday, he was ready to act. At his lunchtime meeting with Clarinda, he asked, "How is Anita?"

"Okay, I think." The question flattened Clarinda's smile. "She's trying so hard to be brave, for my sake, that she's not dealing with her own emotions."

"I know that feeling." The guilt he felt over Johnny going to war multiplied when he saw his parents' grief. "If you don't mind, I'd like to talk with her. You could say we've become friends." What if she objected to Ralph's increasing role in her daughter's life?

"Why would I object?" Clarinda smiled. "If you can help her not be so sad, I'm happy."

"Good. I have one question, though. Do you mind if we start a victory garden behind your house?"

"No. Is that what you have in mind?"

"I hope you like carrots, potatoes and squash." He smiled. "Please give this to Anita. She can tell you whether it's a yes or no."

Clarinda took the envelope, which was opened. "May I read it?"

"Of course."

"'All girls with the initials A.F. are invited to join R.Q. in the back of the Bailey Mansion to help with the war effort at eight o'clock sharp on Saturday morning.'"

Clarinda grinned. "The initials are a nice touch."

"I thought so."

Ralph felt fairly confident that Anita would join him, but just in case, he arrived early, an extra doughnut in his bag in place of breakfast.

"Good morning, Ralph. Glad you're here early—you can join us for breakfast. We're having blueberry pancakes."

Over the table, Clarinda pulled a small card out of a box shaped like a loaf of bread and handed it to Anita. "Read it for us."

"'Put on the whole armor of God, that ye may be able to stand against the wiles of the devil. Ephesians 6:11.'" Anita wrinkled her nose. "The Bible talks about fighting a lot."

"What is the armor of God?" Clarinda asked.

What was this, Bible quiz hour?

"The breastplate of righteousness, feet shod with the gospel of peace, the shield of faith, the helmet of salvation and the sword of the Spirit," Anita promptly answered, as if she had the words memorized. Coming from the Finch family, she probably did. "I know it's not talking an army like Howie and Arthur are in. But why did Jesus say He gave us peace when He tells us to put on armor?" She poured syrup over her pancakes, almost flooding the plate. "Why does God let good men like Dad die?"

Color fled Clarinda's face. Ralph felt the packets of seed in his pocket. "People have been asking that question ever since God let Satan tempt Job. Why do good people suffer?" He cleared his throat. "My brother died during the last war. He was younger even than Arthur, only a few

months older than Betty." He looked at Clarinda, who nodded, as if giving him approval to go ahead.

"It won't make the bad things go away, but I have an idea.
Something you could do to help the war effort, that would
help bring other fathers and husbands and brothers—"

"And sisters," Norma said.

"And sisters," Ralph added. "Help them to come home
sooner. I went to the store and bought every kind of seed
Mr. Adams sells. I thought that together we could grow a
victory garden."

"So that's what the invitation was all about." Anita still
scowled, but she reached out her hand. "What did you
get?" She stared at the assorted packets. "I *hate* turnips."

"But I love them," Clarinda said. "Will you grow some
for me?" Ralph had discussed his plan with Clarinda, and
she had agreed.

The women squabbled over which vegetables to grow—
deciding to try all of them, because maybe some of the
women in the dorm would like them—while Ralph listened good-naturedly.

"What about you, Mr. Quincy?" Anita bounced out
of her chair. "Are you going to help us with the garden?"

"If you have time, we'd love your help." Clarinda's smile
included him in the family. "Please do help us. If you have
time."

Clarinda's invitation was all Ralph needed to hear. "Do
you want to start today? I brought a rake, shovel, spades
and even some gloves."

"Makes me wish I was wearing something suitable for
gardening." Clarinda ran her hands down her light blue
skirt. "We'll meet you after we've changed to something
more appropriate for digging in the dirt."

Ralph waited in the parlor, fingering one packet of seed
he had kept in his pocket, a wildflower mix that Rich

promised would grow well in Vermont's soil. He had cleared a corner of the flower bed for the surprise. When Anita clattered down the hall first, Ralph stood. "I want to show you something before the others get back."

She followed him out the door to a corner of the garden he had prepared earlier that day. "I got this little place ready early this morning. I want you to help me plant it and keep it a secret from your mother. Can you do that?"

"You want to plant something and not tell Mom what it is?"

Ralph nodded. "Let me show you what I have in mind."

After Anita exclaimed over the beautiful picture on the seed packet, he showed her how to turn over the dirt he had tilled earlier that day. "Now you poke a hole in the dirt, a couple of inches down." After a good fifteen minutes, they had planted enough seed to guarantee a lovely array of colors.

Ralph placed his hands on his knees, where he sat on the ground. "Now tell me what we just did."

"We made holes, put the seed in, then covered them up and watered them." Anita didn't quite roll her eyes, but she might as well have. Her bearing suggested any farmer's daughter knew such things.

"What's going to happen to the seed?"

"The stalk will push its head through the dirt."

Ralph shook his head. "Before that."

Anita scratched her head.

"Where does the plant start?"

"Oh, inside the seed."

She was almost there.

"Some people say the seed has to die before the plant can grow. Jesus even described it that way, in John 12:24. Do you know that verse?" Ralph asked.

"I don't think so."

"He said, 'Except a corn of wheat fall into the ground and die, it abideth alone; but if it die, it bringeth forth much fruit.'"

Anita patted the ground where they had planted the seed. "Daddy always said that verse when I helped him plant."

Ralph swallowed. "I'm sure your father would agree with me. He might have gone to heaven, but he's still alive, in you, in your sisters and your brothers."

Anita considered that. "Then what about you, Mr. Quincy? How will you live on after you die, since you don't have any children?"

Chapter 15

When Clarinda came outside, she worked in a different section of the garden, since she sensed Ralph wanted a private chat with Anita. She heard the discussion about the seed dying to bring forth more fruit. It was a good object lesson.

Anita's question about Ralph's lack of children spurred Clarinda into action. She walked over, smiling. "What are you two doing over here in the flower garden?" She used a bright tone, but she didn't fool anyone, least of all herself.

"Anita asked me a question that deserves an answer." Ralph had taken the question in stride, and Clarinda relaxed. This couldn't be the first time someone had asked about his unmarried, childless status.

"No, it doesn't. Anita, you should know better." Clarinda wouldn't allow Anita's rudeness to remain unaddressed.

"Friends can ask each other anything. Isn't that right, Mr. Quincy?"

"You may not always get an answer. But I don't mind the question. Instead of giving me a wife and children of my own, God has given me hundreds of children to look out for, in my classes. I like to think I've made a difference in their lives, and a part of me lives on through them."

Thank you, Ralph, for finding the words. Thank you for helping Anita in the loss of her father, something I have failed to do. Thank you for helping me every step of the way. The words thundered in Clarinda's mind, pushed out of the way by a realization as heady as air that had turned to steam in the heat.

I love Ralph.

The thought rampaged from the toes of her sandaled feet to the kerchief she wore to cover her head. Her feelings must be branded on her forehead, but no one said a thing, as if it was just another Saturday morning in Maple Notch.

"That's good." His answer had satisfied Anita.

"I was thinking we could put the beans over here next to the fence." Ralph walked Clarinda through the plot, suggesting where to plant watermelons and pumpkins and everything else. At least she assumed that was what he was saying. The words flying through her head consisted of things like love and joy, sunshine and warmth, comfort and peace.

How Ralph could remain so near her and not know how she felt seemed impossible. What thoughts hid behind his helpful exterior? Was it possible all the time they had spent together the past six months had more to it than supporting the war effort and leading their town?

Ralph left her side to help Norma with the potato eyes she was planting. His question challenged Norma's math skills. "If an ear of corn has an average of seven hundred kernels on the cob, how many kernels do you like to eat for supper?"

"Two times seven hundred would be…fourteen plus two zeros—1,400!" Norma's math grades had grown steadily better, thanks to his help. Even Anita had benefited from his gift for teaching, and she wasn't even in junior high school yet.

Could he want—to join *her* family?

Did she want him to? *All the children are mine.* But did he care about *Clarinda?* Would he be as…attentive… to her needs, if she wasn't the mayor? The mother of two of his students? The strongest opposition to some of his plans? Perhaps he only wanted to draw attention away from their differences.

Hearing his laugh, watching the shake of his head, Clarinda doubted it. He was genuine through and through. Howard had had a hard time putting his feelings into words. Ralph didn't. He told her up front and listened to her answers.

Howard had been the husband the twenty-two-year-old Clarinda Tuttle had needed. But the longer she worked with Ralph, she questioned if *he* was the husband Mayor Clarinda Tuttle Finch wanted.

"…when the tomatoes are ripe, I'll help you harvest the vegetables if you want me to."

Clarinda's heart warmed at the thought. Ralph planned on staying around her home for the next few months or so, long enough to see the harvest in.

They worked with a will, and Clarinda didn't notice the passage of time until she saw her shadow on the ground, shortened by the noontime sun. Ralph straightened at the same time, rubbing his back. "Are you ready to quit?"

Clarinda shook her head. "There's only one more row. We can work from opposite ends."

How appropriate that they planted succotash, one of the same crops her ancestors had planted when they lived in a cave. The quilt featured a field much like the garden they were planting.

"I'll get lunch started." Anita went inside. Norma had already left for her shift in the nursery, leaving Clarinda and Ralph alone in the garden.

Each time Clarinda glanced up, Ralph did the same thing. After a couple of accidental meetings of their gazes, they made a game of it. Like babies playing peekaboo, the two of them grinned and laughed.

They met in the middle, Ralph's head slightly above Clarinda's. The laughter in his eyes leaped into something more serious, and he leaned forward.

She raised her head in permission, while he pressed the gentlest of butterfly kisses on her lips.

"What just happened?" Clarinda looked at Ralph, her face soft, smoothed by the midday sun.

"I don't know." Ralph had no intentions of kissing Clarinda when he had arrived at the house that morning. Rich's question taunted him. *Are you and the mayor an item?* "But I want to do it again." He leaned forward again and captured Clarinda's lips, savoring the coffee and maple syrup he tasted from breakfast.

When they parted, Ralph held her hands, their foreheads touching, staring at the place where their fingers were joined. The kiss had crossed some boundary between them, one neither of them expected.

"Lunch is ready," Anita yelled through an open window. Had she seen the kiss—make that the *kisses?*

Probably not, or else she wouldn't announce lunch so casually. Whether he and Clarinda could pretend nothing had happened, he didn't know. After standing, he helped Clarinda to her feet. He leaned forward and whispered,

"I meant every pulse of that kiss, but now isn't the best time to discuss it."

Her laugh sounded more like a groan. "Is there ever a good time to discuss personal matters these days?"

He grinned. "At your office. At noon on Monday."

When Ralph hung up the phone on Sunday night, he allowed himself a long sigh. He and Clarinda wouldn't get that time on Monday after all. Betty, on plane-spotter duty, had called with unexpected news. "Mr. Quincy. A Flying Fortress just flew overhead."

As close as they were to the border, they saw Canadian planes frequently. "I'm sure it's routine."

"That's the problem. The plane was headed downward at a steep angle. I'm afraid it…crashed…sir."

Ralph came to attention. "What was the heading?"

When Betty told him, Ralph bit his lip: straight for one of the mountains. This could be bad, truly bad. "Thank you for calling me. You know what to do. I'll take care of things from here."

Ralph called emergency services for the town closest to the plane's trajectory, but his second call went to Clarinda.

The phone rang several times before anyone picked up, but he blamed it on the late hour. "Bedlam Boardinghouse here," Audrey Smith said.

Ralph suppressed a chuckle. Clarinda would *not* appreciate her humor. "This is Mr. Quincy. I need to speak with Mrs. Finch."

"Is something wrong?"

Ralph was about to remind her that the answer was none of her business, when Audrey said, "Never mind. I'll get Mrs. Finch."

Clarinda came on the phone within two minutes.

"Ralph. Audrey said you needed to talk with me. Has something happened?"

"Betty called," Ralph said.

Clarinda gasped, and he hastened to explain. "She's fine, but she spotted a plane going down."

"Have you taken the necessary steps for Maple Notch's safety?" Clarinda asked.

"It was a Canadian Flying Fortress. I called the closest fire department, but I thought you might want to come with me to see it for yourself."

"Of course. I'll call the mayors of the local towns and alert them to a possible emergency landing in the mountains."

Of course Clarinda would know what to do. She really was a good mayor.

Ten minutes later, Clarinda ran out of the house with Hattie at her side.

"Hattie is supposed to relieve Betty at eleven. We'll be taking the highway past the tower, won't we?" Clarinda asked.

Ralph nodded. If the pilot had had any control of the plane, he might choose to land on the tarmac.

"Let's pray for the pilot," Audrey said.

"Please." Clarinda folded her hands in her lap.

All three of them prayed, and silence reigned in the car. "We won't know what to do until we find the plane," Ralph said. Waiting was, always had been, the hardest thing about war.

"Or until we learn he made it to his destination safely. I assume the military authorities are checking with their counterparts in Quebec?"

Ralph nodded. "I have my walkie-talkie. Hattie, I'll call you once we find the pilot. You know who to call after that." He smiled at her. "You have an important job to do tonight."

She straightened her shoulders. When they reached the tower, Hattie knocked on the door before heading up the stairs. Betty appeared a few minutes later.

Betty pointed southwest. "The plane was heading that way." A mountain loomed close, far too close for comfort. "It's so hard to see anything with the blackout, without the plane lights."

Clarinda turned in her daughter's direction. "You should be glad it's dark." She looked at Ralph, and he knew the same thought had crossed her mind.

"Because if the plane had crashed—" Betty's words started slowly than gained momentum. "We would see fire."

No, nothing was lost on the Finch women.

Ralph drove more slowly than he liked, with the twists and turns of the road. Suddenly a light beamed in his face, and he slammed on the brakes. The light was extinguished as quickly as it had appeared.

"Mr. Quincy!"

Ralph recognized the hulking figure that ran in the direction of the car as the deputy constable from the town of Sugar Hill. "We found it. The pilot is alive but can't say much for his plane."

Betty stood on her tiptoes, as if trying to see the pilot.

Clarinda cleared her throat. "I'm sure the rescue workers are taking care of him."

Betty frowned. "But he *is* coming back to Maple Notch, isn't he? Dr. Landrum's clinic is first-rate. He was named as one of the best GPs in all of Vermont."

Clarinda exchanged looks with Ralph. "She *does* have a point. Is he in fit condition to travel?" she asked the deputy.

"The emergency personnel can tell you better than I can. Go ahead and park here."

"I'm fine. Put me on the next bus or a plane and send me back to my unit." A young man in an air force uniform challenged the rescue workers.

"Pilots are *so* brave." Betty looked starstruck, and she hadn't even met the man yet.

"Mr. Quincy, thank you for calling." Sugar Hill's constable shook his hand. Next, he turned to Betty. "And you must be the young woman who brought our attention to this unfortunate accident."

Betty blushed.

The pilot, who was neither old nor ugly but handsome and tall, with wavy blond hair, walked forward. "And who may this vision of loveliness be?"

"I'm Betty, Betty Finch." Clarinda's normally sensible daughter turned into a simpering girl at the sight of the pilot's uniform.

Once again Clarinda rued the day that Betty had signed up with the plane-spotter program. Clarinda had seen the effect of young flying aces on her contemporaries during the Great War, had felt the tug once or twice herself. Betty obviously fell prey to the same hero worship.

Ralph went with the emergency workers to look at the plane while Clarinda and Betty talked with the pilot. His name was Mason Cain. They had his home field wrong. He hailed from Ottawa, not Quebec. "Only by God's grace did I make the road. With the darkness and all the mountains, it was hard to see anything."

"Are you a Christian, then, Captain Cain?" Clarinda asked in her brightest voice. She wanted to remind her daughter of the *most important* quality in a man.

"I certainly am. Paid and saved just a year ago—decided

I better get my life right with God before I started hunting down the enemy."

Betty's smile just grew wider. "You'll have to forgive my mother. She's used to telling people what to do. She's the mayor over in Maple Notch."

Mason turned to Clarinda. "What, you are Miss Finch's mother? I thought you must be her sister."

"Nonsense, Captain. I look every year of my age, and I am not ashamed of it." Still, even she felt the thrill when he lifted her hand and kissed it.

They decided Dr. Landrum was the best physician to check out the young pilot. While they climbed into their cars, another car pulled behind them. Rusty the reporter jumped out, and a flashbulb went off.

"Where is the pilot? You? And, Betty, I understand you called in about the plane? Stand there together so I can get a picture."

Betty stood next to Mason as if she owned him. Clarinda gritted her teeth, reminding herself of the freedom of the press.

"I suppose someone called you," Ralph said.

Rusty grinned in answer. "People like to see good news about the war. This will let people know that the plane-spotter program is making a difference."

They returned home, and in the morning, Dr. Landrum reported that the captain's injuries were more serious than they had first thought. He would remain in Maple Notch for two weeks.

At lunchtime, Ralph headed for Clarinda's office. She was hanging up the phone when he walked in and took his seat across from her. "That was Dr. Landrum. So far, he reports that seven different women have offered to take in Captain Mason, and he asked for my advice. I would have told him we'd take him in, but we have only ladies and a few small boys in residence. I have no desire to be candidate number eight."

Ralph laughed. "Since I am one of the few single men in town, I will extend an invitation. Maybe you and Betty can come up with an excuse to visit. Your daughter appeared quite smitten."

Clarinda scowled but handed the receiver to Ralph while she dialed. He made arrangements and hung up. "Doc says he should be ready to leave the clinic in a couple of days. Seriously, I would love for you and the girls to come for a meal, if he's feeling well enough."

She blinked, opened her mouth and closed it again.

The kiss. Maybe she thought he should bring it up. Maybe he should. He had initiated the impulsive caress, after all. "Clarinda, about the other day…"

"Yes?" Her gaze didn't waver from his face.

His stomach rumbled. He was too old for this. "I never expected to feel this way again, Clarinda. But somewhere along the way, my feelings for you changed from acquaintance to election opponent to admired leader to close friend and now…to something even more. I think I love you. If there was ever a time when we know tomorrow isn't certain, it's now. I don't want to wait any longer."

"Oh, my." Clarinda's face blushed in a whole palette of colors, from white to red to white again. Her eyes wandered over the room, gazing at the windows where anyone could see them at lunch together, to the open door, where Hazel kept an eye on her boss, to the pictures of her family—to the picture of Howard, former mayor as well as late husband.

Ralph held his breath. Little more than a year had passed since Howard had died. Was Clarinda ready for another man to take his place?

At last she looked at him, her brown eyes darkened to

a smoky gray. "Ralph, you have become dear to me, as well. But I don't know—"

The phone rang, and Clarinda grabbed it like a lifeline to save her from answering. "Yes, come in."

The face she turned to Ralph had paled even further than before. "I have a telegram."

Chapter 16

Clarinda's heart flew to her throat while her stomach plummeted. A telegram—every mother's worst fear.

Rich Adams ran the telegraph office out of his store, and he had brought the telegram in person. He seemed—pleased—which Clarinda found odd. "I knew you would want to see this right away." He handed her the thin envelope.

Clarinda took the letter opener from her desk drawer and slipped it under the flap, careful of the paper inside. All too soon she had the envelope open, the paper bearing the unbearable news in her hands. She read it once...twice...and started to laugh.

Rich grinned in response.

"What is it?" Ralph rose out of his chair.

"Howie is *married*." She shook her head. Howie was young enough to make such an impetuous decision, but Ralph... She'd deal with that another time. "And he says 'coming for graduation.'" She clapped her hands together. "My boy is coming home!" She picked up the picture of Howie in uniform and kissed it.

"What's her name?"

"Marjorie Hunt. That's all he said. Maybe he's sending a letter with more details and a picture or *something*." Howie had used minimal words on the telegram. Married to Marjorie Hunt. Coming for graduation. "Oh, I hope he gets to come home." Anticipated leave could be changed in a matter of minutes, in the middle of a war zone. "I have a daughter-in-law." She started laughing again. "A war bride. I have prayed for God to give my children the right husbands and wives since they were little, so I have to believe Miss Marjorie Hunt is God's choice."

Feeling lighter than she had for a while, Clarinda danced around the room, like a bird looking for a place to land. Outside, the sun brightened the lawn, sparkling on the blooming flowers of spring. Her sons were alive; she had a daughter-in-law—and a wonderful man had said he loved her. Her mind skittered away from that.

"Congratulations, Clarinda. I'm so glad it was good news." Ralph prepared to leave with Rich, and she realized that lunchtime was over.

"Don't say a word to my girls."

"Of course not. Norma wouldn't pay any attention in class if I told her now."

After the men left, Clarinda couldn't stop grinning. So Howie had found himself a bride. Every unmarried girl in the boardinghouse would be jealous. Look at the fuss they were all making over Captain Cain.

She hadn't acted much better when Ralph had declared himself today. In a small part in her heart, where logic held no place, a warmth glowed and wanted to grow, to make itself felt. She told herself she should extinguish the flame, but the stubborn flare refused all efforts to snuff it out.

Norma bounced into the office after school. Even now that she had brought up her math grades, she continued stopping by, and Clarinda enjoyed the few minutes alone with her daughter. After finishing a cookie, she said, "Mr. Quincy says you have something to tell me."

"I don't know." Clarinda pretended to consider her answer. "Maybe I should wait until we're all together tonight."

"Mom." Exasperated, Norma broke a second cookie into small pieces.

Clarinda almost said, "I received a telegram today." But the thought of a telegram would terrify her girls as it had frightened her. "I heard from Howie today."

"He sent a letter? Let me see."

"Clean your hands." Clarinda passed the telegraph-office envelope over the desk.

Norma paled when she saw the telegram. She wiped her hands on her napkin and took it, tugging at the paper inside. "He's *married?*"

Clarinda nodded. "It appears you have a sister-in-law."

Norma squealed, but then she slumped in her chair. "I suppose that means Howie won't come back to Maple Notch after the war is over."

"Of course he will." Clarinda wouldn't allow herself to think any differently.

"Oh, Mom. The man leaves his parents and goes wherever his wife lives."

The thought that Howie might not want to farm the land that had been in the Tuttle family for a century and a half sent a pang to Clarinda's heart. "When they come to visit us, we'll just have to convince her that she'll love living here with us."

When the family settled down to work on the quilt that night, Betty echoed the sentiment. "Here she'll be surrounded by all kinds of family. It's perfect."

"One more story to add to the quilt, if we had time." Clarinda smiled. Tonight together they began the laborious process of joining the squares with different scenes from Maple Notch history. She wondered if, in their desire to incorporate as much history as possible, they had aimed too high. Less than a month remained, and the hardest work lay ahead.

"There have been several war brides in our family." Betty stitched together the blocks featuring the capture of the bank robbers at the old Tuttle Bridge with the opening of the seminary. "Think of Grandma Clara and Grandfather Daniel. He fought in the Civil War, and they got married after he returned, and she thought she would remain the town spinster."

So Betty had listened to the stories after all. Clarinda smiled.

"Maybe Captain Cain will fall in love with you and take you to Canada with him." Anita handed the quilt to Clarinda to approve the stitches.

"Never." Betty shook her head. "He's terribly romantic, but I'm going to be a driver in the army. I'm good with cars."

Clarinda's heart jumped into her throat. If left up to her, Betty would marry and live a few hundred miles away rather than running around in Europe with bombs going off and stray bullets flying.

What would her girls say if she told them *she* might be the next war bride?

Ralph opened the city-hall door for Clarinda to exit and slipped his arm through hers as they walked down the marble stairs and paused on the sidewalk to check for traffic. A car passed with one of the high school seniors behind the steering wheel. Slowing down the vehicle, he stuck his head out the window. "Hello there, Mr. Quincy! Mrs. Finch! It's a beautiful day to be outside, isn't it?"

Ralph nodded. "Yes, it is. Now get back to school before your next class begins."

"I will." The kid grinned and put his foot on the accelerator.

"I can't believe I let you talk me into this." Clarinda adjusted her hat farther down her forehead, and Ralph wondered if she wanted to hide her face. But then she raised her head and looked straight forward, a smile on her face. "Rusty could decide to stroll through the town square today to take our picture. We might as well announce it to the world."

Ralph chuckled. "That doesn't bother me. Does it trouble you?"

Clarinda lifted her face to the sky and closed her eyes, soaking in the sun. Taking in a deep breath, she smiled at Ralph. "Not at all. 'God's in His heaven— All's right with the world,' as Browning put it. There is no reason why we can't enjoy such a lovely day outside." She squeezed her fingers where they touched his arm. "Even if tongues wag."

Ralph felt as if he could float across the street. "Where would you like to sit?"

Clarinda eyed the tables sitting in the center of the square, under the shelter of the trees, but then pointed toward a spot in the sun. Shadows could be chilly in mid-May. "As long as we are eating together in public in the middle of the day, we might as well make sure everyone can see us." Her smile suggested she wasn't opposed to the idea. "That is, if you don't mind."

Ralph's grin grew wider. "Not at all, Madam Mayor."

He had packed a blanket in the picnic basket for such a decision. When they reached a sunny spot, he removed the blanket from the basket and unfolded it with a flick of his wrist, and it settled down neatly on the ground. They took places on opposite corners of the blanket, the basket in between them filled with everything Ralph had learned how to cook well over thirty years of bachelor cooking. He offered her dish after dish.

"Please, no more! I can't possibly eat everything I have already."

"You must at least try my apple pie." Ralph grinned. "But I'll make it a small taste." He cut a sliver off the pie he had packed in a bowl and handed it to her on a small plate. "I even have cheese to add to it, if you would like some."

She shook her head.

More people than he had expected, at least half a dozen, walked around and through the town square while the two of them ate. By the time they started on the apple pie, Rich Adams came out the door and waved at them. He crossed the square with long strides, but instead of the smile Ralph expected, his face was somber. "I probably shouldn't tell you this…."

Clarinda looked up sharply at his tone. "What's happened, Rich?"

Rich slapped a telegram envelope on his left palm.

"Bad news?" Ralph's heart crept into his throat. Every casualty reminded both him and Clarinda of their losses. What an ugly thing to mar such a beautiful day.

"I'm afraid so. It's young Everett Lee."

Ralph's mind went black. Everett, who had sat in class less than six months ago, gone. "Any word of young Irving?" *Please say no.*

Rich shook his head. "Not yet."

"I wonder where they were fighting." Clarinda's voice wavered.

Rich looked up. "There is no reason to think they're fighting in the same place as your boys."

"No reason why they're not, either." Clarinda's voice shrilled as she gasped for breath. He had hoped today would provide a break from her constant burdens of family, war and town business, but death brought it back home. She swallowed. "I will come with you as you deliver the news. It will help his mother to have someone else along."

Ralph stood and helped her to her feet. He wanted to kiss her, to hug her, but knew she would resist such a public display. "We'll try again another day."

"It was lovely."

How he loved her smile.

"It gave me a much-needed break," she said.

The next morning, the school buzzed with news of Everett's death. Ralph's secretary followed him into his office, with his cup of coffee and copy of the paper. "Such terrible news, Mr. Quincy."

No work would be accomplished this day. Ralph called a school assembly during second period. All the students filed in, from seventh graders through juniors. The seniors didn't follow the juniors, and Ralph raised a quizzical eyebrow at the senior adviser. He shrugged and left to look for them.

Ralph waited while his secretary passed out a quickly written agenda among the staff. The noise level in the auditorium rose quickly. At last the back door opened, and the seniors walked down the center aisle, side by side, as if they were promenading for graduation. Their arrival, with universally stoic facial expressions, quieted the students. At the back of the line came Betty and Steve, the young man who competed with her for valedictory honors. Between them, they carried a large poster board.

As they took their seats, the back door opened again and Rusty Henshaw came in. His arrival frightened Ralph most of all. What was happening?

Betty whispered in the adviser's ear and he nodded. He joined Ralph on the platform. "Betty and Steve want to speak to the school before we close the session. I told her that would be acceptable."

Ralph guessed that the seniors had formed their own response to the death of one of their own. Now that the room had quieted, he took his place at the podium. The usual preliminaries, reciting the Pledge of Allegiance and singing the national anthem, seemed more important than ever at such a time. "I have called us here together to tell you that Everett Lee, a young man who attended Maple Notch High School until he enlisted in the army earlier this year, was killed in action last week."

Renewed murmurings broke out among the students but quieted when he raised his hand. "I called us here to tell you the truth, and to tell you of the school's plan to honor Mr. Lee. However, I believe our seniors have already chosen a plan of action. Miss Betty Finch and Mr. Steve Roberts, please join me on the platform."

Steve helped Betty up the steps. They strode with such purpose that their demeanor reminded Ralph that they were, in fact, young adults, capable of facing the world on their own.

Betty took the mike first. "I haven't seen much of Everett since grade school, but I remember him as a kind boy, someone who made sure everyone on the playground got their turns on the equipment. But I do know what it's like to lose somebody you love in this war." Her voice wobbled. "So I asked the other seniors about what we'd like to do to honor Everett."

Betty helped Steve lift the poster board into the air. Steve said, "All the seniors signed this pact, every one of us, in honor of Everett Lee."

Betty read from the poster. "In honor of Everett Lee, we, the seniors of Maple Notch High School, do pledge..."

No, don't say it. The words lodged in Ralph's throat.

"...to enlist in one of the branches of the military the day after our graduation next month."

The back door opened, and a swatch of light poured over the gathering. Clarinda appeared, stumbling down the middle aisle, tears streaming down her face, as if she was unaware of anyone around her. Ralph saw a telegram in her hand and left the platform. "What is it?" he asked urgently.

"It's Arthur. He's missing in action." She collapsed in his arms while Betty and Norma raced to her side.

Chapter 17

The four Finch women gathered in the sewing room to put the finishing touches on their quilt. Clarinda's hand shook as she worked on the final quilting block, the one that listed the names of the men either killed, missing in action or taken prisoner from Maple Notch. *Howard Finch Sr. Everett Lee. Arthur Finch.*

She wanted to rage at God, to question His plan to take both her husband and her son. Instead, as mayor and mother, she kept up a brave face, saying Arthur was only missing. He would return home safe and sound, that missing in action was far better than killed. Only in private, or with Ralph, did she allow her mask to fall.

The long hours spent quilting had offered a mindless opiate, allowing her to stay busy without thinking overmuch, to reassure the girls in their worry and grief. The ladies had decided to hold the auction on the Saturday before Memorial Day, in honor of those who'd died.

Clarinda treasured these weeks with the girls. Betty would leave all too soon. She remained firm in her resolve to enlist in the Women's Army Corps the day after graduation. Until then, she spent as much time as possible with her aunt Mary Anne, a good mechanic, coming home covered in dirt and oil more often than not.

Ralph had offered a second training class for people involved in plane spotting. He allowed a few underclassmen to train, promising their parents that an adult would sit with them. Norma, of course, had jumped at the opportunity, and soon took over many of Betty's hours in the tower.

Anita spent a lot of free time in the garden, nurturing the new plants—that was, when she wasn't busy collecting tin and glass and keeping detailed records of all her activities. That one would be a writer someday; Clarinda knew it.

She was with her girls now, all sewing. A teardrop formed beneath Clarinda's eyelid, and she dabbed at it with a handkerchief. She didn't want to ruin the quilt with salty residue on the eve of the auction.

Betty pulled her needle through the material, secured the thread and cut the end. "This corner is done."

Clarinda finished next, followed by Norma and Anita. They cleared the floor and spread out the quilt. If Clarinda said so herself, they had done quality work, but the purpose of the quilts, all of which were certain to be beautiful, was to raise money, after all.

"I can't wait to see the other quilts," Anita said.

Norma scoffed. "I've seen the one they're working on at school—it's set up in the home-ec room. Ours is lots better."

Clarinda made a tsking sound, but secretly she was pleased, and she bet the girls knew it, too.

"Good." Anita giggled.

The residents came to inspect the final product a moment before the doorbell rang. *Ralph.* Clarinda's heart sped up. He waited outside, wearing a blue short-sleeved chambray shirt, his hair cut in an attempt to keep the curls under control.

She opened the door. "I'm not sure if I recognize you without your suit on."

"Maybe this will remind you." He kissed her on the cheek.

A giggle behind them told Clarinda that Anita was watching. Ralph called over Clarinda's shoulder, "Is the quilt ready?"

"Come and see!" Anita led Ralph by the hand into the parlor, where the twenty-five-square quilt was laid out.

Ralph walked around the quilt. "There are ice skates, for Frank and Winnie, both of them our national gold medal winners."

"Of course."

"And the time the mob decided to run gin through our town, and Wallace and Mary Anne helped put a stop to it."

"Yes."

"In fact, every scene on this quilt has something to do with your family." He reached the last square and his smile disappeared. "Howard, Everett, Arthur." He shook his head. "We're praying Arthur home. The whole town is."

He patted her shoulder awkwardly, but she knew his feelings ran deep.

"I know. Thank you."

"The quilt is indeed beautiful. It should fetch a pretty penny tomorrow."

The women folded the quilt, and Ralph helped wrap brown paper around the thick bundle. "You can let go of this. I'll take care of it."

Clarinda knew he was talking about more than the quilt. The church sanctuary filled by midmorning on Saturday. Ralph brought the auctioneer around, introducing him to all the different quilting guilds "so no one can make charges of special treatment," he said.

For her part, Clarinda made the rounds of the room, studying each quilt. The designs couldn't have been more different. One quilt featured a star pattern in shades of red, white and blue; another group had stitched the various flags that had flown over the town through the years. Quilts featuring the insignias of each branch of the service and the planes the plane spotters looked for, with the plane-spotter insignia in the center, rounded out the lot. As a whole, they were a breathtaking array of creativity and color and design, worthy of the auction, and she told all the ladies so.

She spotted a familiar face at the door, and a smile sprang to her face. The mayor of St. Albans had come with his wife. As Clarinda glanced around the room, she recognized dignitaries from most of the towns in Chittenden County and a few seminary graduates from farther afield. She walked up and down the rows, greeting old friends and welcoming them to town before settling down for the bidding to start.

By the time the auction finished at twelve-thirty, more than $10,000 had been raised for the war effort.

Well done, ladies. All the women of Maple Notch had come together on this project, from her Rosie Riveters to the oldest widow and everyone in between. Grandma Clara would be proud.

Six days after the success of the quilt auction, Ralph faced the proudest and hardest day of the year: graduation. He found it difficult to say goodbye to the students he had shepherded on their journey through awkward adolescence to responsible maturity.

In twenty-five years of teaching, he had never had an entire class enlist in the army as soon as they had their diplomas in hand. They were leaving Maple Notch like sacrificial lambs, and he could only pray their blood wouldn't be spilled.

Fifty students marched in pairs, with Betty and Steve as valedictorian and salutatorian of the class of '43. From Ralph's spot on the platform, he saw that Clarinda turned around several times. And Ralph knew why. Howard had promised to attend Betty's graduation, and he had not yet arrived. With Arthur still missing in action, every minute's delay moved with agonizing slowness.

The ceremony began with the presentation of awards—including a new award, the Maple Notch Female Seminary scholarship for the graduating female with the highest grade point average, funded by the Finch and Tuttle families. Ralph smiled as he announced the award, pausing for a moment's reflection on the changes the past year had brought. In the program, he had written:

> It is fitting that the tradition of the Maple Notch Female Seminary be honored with a scholarship for each year's female student with the highest average. Clara Farley Tuttle's legacy lives on.

Clarinda smiled her first genuine smile of the day, and Ralph was pleased he could ease her in some way.

"Huzzah!" came a call at the back of the auditorium. Betty's hand flew to her mouth after a startled cry came out. Howard had arrived, a lovely young woman by his side.

"Continue on." A grinning Howard saluted Ralph and took a seat.

Ralph admired Betty's presence of mind to present her

passionate graduation address without benefit of notes in spite of Howard's last-minute arrival. Soon the final remarks were finished, and the ceremony concluded. Betty flew down the aisle, Ralph following at a slower pace, stopping to congratulate parents and students alike. He passed a couple of boys making plans to drive to the marine recruiting station together in the morning. His heart hammered in his chest, but he would leave them in God's hands. That was all he—or anyone else—could do.

After he said hello to another graduate—a young woman he had doubted would ever graduate, who was now entering the WAVES—he headed for the Finch family gathering. In addition to Clarinda's children, her brother, Wallace, and his wife, Mary Anne, had joined the celebration. Former flapper Mary Anne had taken Betty under her wing, pouring everything she knew about engines into her niece. Wallace, as the author of three respected books about wildlife in Vermont, might be just the person to guide Anita's interest in writing. Who knew where God would lead Norma or any of them? None of them could count beyond today.

Howard had matured greatly during his ten-month absence. His wife was as proud of him as he was of her—that much was clear on their faces. He motioned Ralph forward.

"Marjorie, this is Mr. Quincy, our high school principal. Although you were still a lowly history teacher when you taught me world history during my senior year." Howard grasped his hand, practically grinding his bones.

"So, indulge me. Tell me the story." Ralph asked the question on everyone's mind.

"Smile." A light flashed in Howard's direction, and Rusty Henshaw stepped forward. "I want to hear your story, too, so I can tell all of your curious neighbors."

"Let me guess. You must be Rusty Henshaw, the newspaperman." Marjorie's voice was pure Midwest, but her smile spoke a universal language. "Howard has told me so much about Maple Notch. I feel like I know all of you already."

"We'll have to get back to you on that, Mr. Henshaw." Howard wrapped his arm around Marjorie in a protective hug. "Family first. I'm sure you understand."

Rusty backed away. "I'll call sometime this weekend."

Ralph stuck out his hand in an effort to say goodbye, but Howard grabbed his hand with a firm shake. "I do hope you plan on coming with us. From what I hear, you're almost a part of the family." His tone was friendly, but his hazel eyes, so like his father's, demanded an accounting.

Clarinda blushed at that statement. "Mr. Quincy might have other plans for the day, Howie—Howard, I mean."

"Nope." Ralph grinned. "I'm hoping for a chance to speak with Howard myself."

Howard answered with a grin.

Having Howard and Wallace with them at the dinner table provided a nice balance in the usually all-female household. Ralph didn't say much, content to listen and absorb the flow of conversation.

They had cleared the dinner plates when Howard stood to his feet. "We have news to report. We were wondering— Marjorie and I—if Marjorie can stay with you when I leave this time. Her father's in the army, and her mother has just moved into a tiny apartment."

"Of course." Clarinda stood and hugged her daughter-in-law. "You know you don't have to ask."

"Thank you." Marjorie hugged Clarinda back.

"She needs a mom more than ever because—" For the first time since Howard had arrived home, he appeared ill at ease.

"Because I'm expecting a baby." Marjorie's joy and pride made itself felt in her voice.

"Congratulations." Ralph's response was swallowed by Anita's exuberant shout.

As the afternoon wore on, Ralph wondered how he was going to separate Clarinda from her children long enough to speak to them alone. He decided to enlist Betty's help, since she already knew his secret. "Can you get your mother out of here for a few minutes? I need to ask your brother and sisters a question."

"*The* question?" Betty's eyes sparkled. "Of course."

Before Ralph knew it, Betty had swept her mother and Marjorie out of the room on a pretext of looking for baby furniture. As they left, she winked at Ralph.

He didn't know how long they would be gone—and he stood in front of Howard, Norma and Anita, speechless. He cleared his throat.

Howard chuckled, and he wiped at his eyes. "I'm sorry. I can't help it. You look the way I felt when I went to Mr. Hunt. Except I had only known Marjorie for a month."

"Are you going to marry Mom?" Anita squealed.

"Shh." Norma put a finger to her lips. "He doesn't want Mom to know."

Ralph felt deflated. "You all *know?*"

Norma shrugged her shoulders. "I guessed, when Betty started acting all mysterious and smiling when she saw the two of you together."

"She wrote to me about it." Howard reached out his hand. "Welcome to our family."

"So I gather I have your permission to ask your mother to marry me?" Relief coated Ralph's insides like warm honey.

"I'm glad to see her with a good man," Howard said. Norma and Anita nodded their heads.

"Then the only thing that remains to do is to ask the lady herself."

"The answer is yes." Clarinda took one step forward and then ran into Ralph's arms, where she belonged.

Epilogue

"Mom, you're *beautiful*." Anita had grown over the summer until she was nearly as tall as Clarinda. She kissed her mother on the cheek.

Clarinda wasn't so sure. "We might be the oddest-looking bridal party our church has ever seen." Betty would wear her WAC uniform, the fashionable thigh-length jacket over a straight skirt but in that ugly olive shade. Clarinda had decided to wear a lilac blouse—it might be almost fall, but why not wear her favorite color? In planning dresses for Marjorie, Norma and Anita, they chose rainbow colors, all of them in a similar style to Betty's uniform, except for Anita's jumper.

The Finches had spent most of their fabric coupons on completing the quilt, so Clarinda was delighted when her family and townspeople combined resources to give her a new outfit for her wedding. Clarinda fingered the ribbed binding to her blouse, with short, puffed sleeves and violet piping, over a calf-length gray skirt, which she could wear on other occasions, as well. She refused to wear a dress only one time.

Betty pinned her hat on before she helped Clarinda with her hat and veil. The young woman standing in front of Clarinda looked confident and beautiful. "The hat makes the uniform," Clarinda said.

"Do you think so?" Betty asked.

Clarinda closed her mind to the dozens of young men who would find her daughter alluring. She had given each of her children to God before they were born—even Arthur. Her hopes for his eventual return grew smaller and smaller with each passing day. And now Betty was ready to leave boot camp and join the fight, as well.

Norma dashed to the kitchen and came back with Clarinda's bouquet, lovely red roses that matched the sentiment of the occasion if not the dress.

Rich Adams would join Clarinda's brother and brother-in-law as groomsmen. Frank and Winnie had made the trip to Maple Notch from Boston, where Frank worked as an ice-skating coach. Ralph decided to leave the title of "best man" empty. "It belongs to Johnny."

Clarinda understood completely.

Mary Anne poked her head around the door. "Are you ladies almost ready?" Even though they said yes, she slipped around the door into the room. "I have something for you, Clarinda. Something old—or maybe something new—it depends on how you look at it." She handed Clarinda a jewelry box.

Puzzled, Clarinda opened the box and found a wooden cross on a gold chain. "It's lovely, but you didn't need to give me anything."

"We wanted to." She wrapped Clarinda's fingers around the cross. "You may not know it, but every time Wallace finds a piece of the old bridge, he brings it home. If you look closely at that piece, it has an initial on it. It's from the courting plank—we're sure of it."

Clarinda turned the cross over and found the initial. "It's a *C*."

"It might even have belonged to Grandma Clara." Mary Anne smiled.

With the revelation of the necklace's origins, Clarinda's opinion reversed direction, and she fastened it around her neck, where it dangled between the turned edges of her collar.

Outside the window, a car door slammed, and Clarinda wondered who was nearly late to the wedding. A minute later, someone knocked on the door to their room.

"Who is it?" Betty called. She had been fierce about not allowing Ralph and Clarinda to see each other before the ceremony.

"Almost a stranger."

It couldn't be…or could it?

The door opened a crack. "Are you dressed for company?"

Betty's hand flew to her mouth, and she yanked the door open. "Arthur!"

Thin—oh, so thin. Skin leathered by days in the elements. But her son managed to have the same saucy grin as ever. Clarinda opened her arms in speechless invitation, and he moved into her embrace.

"I'll tell the organist that you'll be a few minutes." Mary Anne left the room.

Norma, Anita and Betty crowded around their brother, each one of them claiming their own piece of him. Marjorie hung back. Clarinda stepped back, her arms still resting on Arthur's shoulder. "Arthur, you must meet your sister-in-law, Marjorie."

Marjorie was openly crying.

"So Howie went and found himself a dame. Pleased to meet you, Marjorie."

Mary Anne came back in. "Are you ready yet?"

"May I escort you down the aisle?" Arthur asked.

"I will be offended if you don't," Clarinda said. "How did you know about—" she gestured around "—all this. The wedding?"

"The man who drove me up here is involved with the plane spotters. He had heard it from Mr. Quincy."

Clarinda had many more questions but they would keep for now.

Mary Anne nodded as if satisfied and left the room. Anita left the room next, taking her place at the entrance to the sanctuary, followed by Norma, Marjorie and Betty, as her maid of honor.

"It's a good thing Dr. Landrum is here." Clarinda patted Arthur's arm.

"Why is that?" he asked.

"In case someone faints when they see you."

Anita started down the aisle. Clarinda brushed her forehead, seeking a curl that wasn't there. How different this wedding was from the one twenty-five years ago. How different the men were.

Clarinda waited hidden from view for the strains of the wedding march. The first chord sounded, and Arthur said, "Here comes the bride."

They stepped in unison as if they had rehearsed it. Clarinda knew people around her must be gasping, but she only looked at the triumphant smile on Ralph's face.

Ralph might not have won the election—but the mayor's heart belonged to him.

Nothing could please her—or Maple Notch—more.

* * * * *

REQUEST YOUR FREE BOOKS!

2 FREE INSPIRATIONAL NOVELS
PLUS 2
FREE
MYSTERY GIFTS

Love Inspired

YES! Please send me 2 FREE Love Inspired® novels and my 2 FREE mystery gifts (gifts are worth about $10). After receiving them, if I don't wish to receive any more books, I can return the shipping statement marked "cancel." If I don't cancel, I will receive 6 brand-new novels every month and be billed just $4.74 per book in the U.S. or $5.24 per book in Canada. That's a savings of at least 21% off the cover price. It's quite a bargain! Shipping and handling is just 50¢ per book in the U.S. and 75¢ per book in Canada.* I understand that accepting the 2 free books and gifts places me under no obligation to buy anything. I can always return a shipment and cancel at any time. Even if I never buy another book, the two free books and gifts are mine to keep forever.

105/305 IDN F49N

Name	(PLEASE PRINT)
Address	Apt. #
City	State/Prov.	Zip/Postal Code

Signature (if under 18, a parent or guardian must sign)

Mail to the **Harlequin® Reader Service:**
IN U.S.A.: P.O. Box 1867, Buffalo, NY 14240-1867
IN CANADA: P.O. Box 609, Fort Erie, Ontario L2A 5X3

**Are you a subscriber to Love Inspired books
and want to receive the larger-print edition?
Call 1-800-873-8635 or visit www.ReaderService.com.**

* Terms and prices subject to change without notice. Prices do not include applicable taxes. Sales tax applicable in N.Y. Canadian residents will be charged applicable taxes. Offer not valid in Quebec. This offer is limited to one order per household. Not valid for current subscribers to Love Inspired books. All orders subject to credit approval. Credit or debit balances in a customer's account(s) may be offset by any other outstanding balance owed by or to the customer. Please allow 4 to 6 weeks for delivery. Offer available while quantities last.

Your Privacy—The Harlequin® Reader Service is committed to protecting your privacy. Our Privacy Policy is available online at www.ReaderService.com or upon request from the Harlequin Reader Service.
We make a portion of our mailing list available to reputable third parties that offer products we believe may interest you. If you prefer that we not exchange your name with third parties, or if you wish to clarify or modify your communication preferences, please visit us at www.ReaderService.com/consumerschoice or write to us at Harlequin Reader Service Preference Service, P.O. Box 9062, Buffalo, NY 14269. Include your complete name and address.

LIDIR13R

REQUEST YOUR FREE BOOKS!

2 FREE INSPIRATIONAL NOVELS
PLUS 2
FREE
MYSTERY GIFTS

Love Inspired.
HISTORICAL
INSPIRATIONAL HISTORICAL ROMANCE

YES! Please send me 2 FREE Love Inspired® Historical novels and my 2 FREE mystery gifts (gifts are worth about $10). After receiving them, if I don't wish to receive any more books, I can return the shipping statement marked "cancel." If I don't cancel, I will receive 4 brand-new novels every month and be billed just $4.74 per book in the U.S. or $5.24 per book in Canada. That's a savings of at least 21% off the cover price. It's quite a bargain! Shipping and handling is just 50¢ per book in the U.S. and 75¢ per book in Canada.* I understand that accepting the 2 free books and gifts places me under no obligation to buy anything. I can always return a shipment and cancel at any time. Even if I never buy another book, the two free books and gifts are mine to keep forever.

102/302 IDN F5CY

Name	(PLEASE PRINT)

Address	Apt. #

City	State/Prov.	Zip/Postal Code

Signature (if under 18, a parent or guardian must sign)

Mail to the Harlequin® Reader Service:
IN U.S.A.: P.O. Box 1867, Buffalo, NY 14240-1867
IN CANADA: P.O. Box 609, Fort Erie, Ontario L2A 5X3

Want to try two free books from another series?
Call 1-800-873-8635 or visit www.ReaderService.com.

* Terms and prices subject to change without notice. Prices do not include applicable taxes. Sales tax applicable in N.Y. Canadian residents will be charged applicable taxes. Offer not valid in Quebec. This offer is limited to one order per household. Not valid for current subscribers to Love Inspired Historical books. All orders subject to credit approval. Credit or debit balances in a customer's account(s) may be offset by any other outstanding balance owed by or to the customer. Please allow 4 to 6 weeks for delivery. Offer available while quantities last.

Your Privacy—The Harlequin® Reader Service is committed to protecting your privacy. Our Privacy Policy is available online at www.ReaderService.com or upon request from the Harlequin Reader Service.

We make a portion of our mailing list available to reputable third parties that offer products we believe may interest you. If you prefer that we not exchange your name with third parties, or if you wish to clarify or modify your communication preferences, please visit us at www.ReaderService.com/consumerschoice or write to us at Harlequin Reader Service Preference Service, P.O. Box 9062, Buffalo, NY 14269. Include your complete name and address.

LIHDIR13R